LIBRARI
WITHDRAWN FR

THis book is interactive
PRESS HERE
TO SKIP INTRO
(then turn to page 12)

Once, up on a lime-green chair, there was a girl called Thomasina Ginger. That's me. You can call me Tom, everyone else does. That or just "Braces".

That's why I'm here – braces. I'm getting new ones fitted. The green chair is a dentist's chair. The first time we meet and you can see right down to my tonsils. I have close friends who haven't seen so much of me. Actually, I don't. Have close friends. Not really.

TOM GINGER (ME)
AKA BRACES

FIONA WISDOM
DENTIST

The other person in the room is the dentist, Fiona Wisdom. She says I can call her just "Fiona", but I never do. I can open up to her ... but mostly when I have to say "Aaaaaaaaah". I'd like to be able to say more. Would like to talk to anyone more, to be honest.

"AAAAAAH!" says Mum.

Mum is the other person in the room – sat in the corner. She's not having a brace put in or anything, though; she's here with me. Although as ever, she's busy with her phone. She's ALWAYS busy with her phone.

The phone makes a tinkly, sparkly noise. "YESSS!" Mum hisses. She must be playing Fruit Fantasy 3 – it's one of her favourite games. Her phone is her pride and joy, especially since she got her latest upgrade. I can't compete.

MUM
AKA @GINGERNINJA_88

Fruit Fantasy
Games
Kill time – the zesty way!
★★★★★ (527)

Buy now

I hear the sound effect for a pineapple exploding. Mum smiles at the screen.

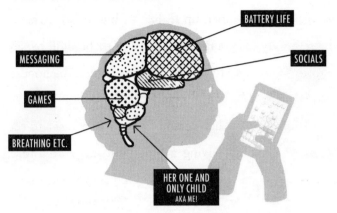

I've had braces for ages. These new ones are called MegaByte-2000s. They're pretty basic. I'd much rather get those invisible ones. These have more of a "classic" design (by which I mean rubbish). They make me look like I've eaten a KitKat and forgotten to unwrap it first.

Once the fitting's over, Fiona gives me a bunch of special dentist stickers. I stick them all in my Filofax, where I keep this kind of thing.

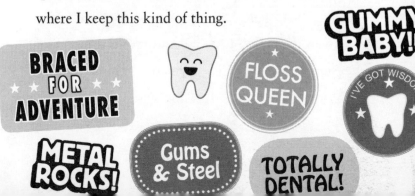

I was hardly Connie McConfidence before, but now … I mean, sure, my braces make me more attractive – but only to magnets. If those stickers told the truth about me, they would be a lot less jolly.

On the noticeboard in the waiting room, there's a poster that says, "Hey, kids, flossing is cool now!" with dancing stick-figures. It's kind of funny. I point it out to Mum, but she's still distracted by her fruit game.

"Now, you're going to have to come back for regular check-ups, so I can see how you and the braces are getting on," Fiona says. "You've got to care for them. And there are certain things you can't eat: peanuts, pistachios, hazelnuts, cashews, macadamias – basically all nuts. Just stay away from them. I do. I'm sure your mum will help you out." Fiona looks up at Mum. "Won't you, Mrs Ginger?"

"Mmm," grunts Mum, without taking her eyes off her phone.

Fiona frowns a little but then goes on. "And no chewing gum. Or toffee apples."

"NUTS!" Mum shouts suddenly, making Fiona jump.

"Er ... yes, good point," Fiona says, nodding. "Thanks. I already said nuts, but they really are the worst of all, so it's worth repeating. No nuts!"

NO
NUTS

NO
CHEWING GUM

NO
FUNFAIR FOOD

NO
BROCCOLI

↑
NOT A BRACES THING, IT'S JUST HORRIBLE

Mum sighs and presses PAUSE on her game. "I'm sorry," she says, looking up from the screen at last. "What are you on about?" The lenses of her glasses reflect the candy colours of her glowing screen. "This really isn't a good time for me to talk about—" She wafts a hand in my general direction, "kid stuff. I'm up to the pomegranates over here." (It's a Fruit Fantasy thing.)

"O–K," says Fiona slowly, clearly a little confused. "It's just this is quite important stuff, for your daughter's dental health."

"OK, OK. Hold on a minute," Mum says. "Just say it into this, will you?" She holds up her phone. The screen is filled with the big red circle of the voice memo app. "Go on," she says. "Say all that stuff again, so Thomasina can remember it. How many toffee apples is it? And is that per day, or what?"

Oh crumbs, this is embarrassing. Fiona is a little shocked, but she goes ahead and repeats everything she's just said into the phone.

Mum plays it back so we can all hear. A robotic version of Fiona's voice comes out of the tiny speaker.

"Well, erm, I was just saying that with these braces, Thomasina will need to stay away from nuts and chewing gum—"

Mum cuts the playback short. "Blah, blah, blah… There, we have it, all recorded. And I can play it back with auto-tune, so it sounds like a rap song. Do you want to hear it?"

Fiona looks even more shocked. She's clearly not used to this style of parenting. "I should probably get to my next patient," she says.

That was weird, right? I want to say to Fiona, to show that I'm normal. I want to say it, but I can't.

"Phones are brilliant, aren't they?" says Mum. "What a time to be alive!"

Fiona looks back at me, smiling a supportive smile: all pearly white teeth and confidence. "Just remember," she says. "No ifs, no buts: no gum, no nuts. Stick with that and you'll be grand." She smiles again. "You'll be the same Thomasina Ginger you've always been."

NO IFS,
NO BUTS:
NO GUM
AND
NO NUTS

Oh, great...

WALKER
BOOKS

MY HEAD

EV

GEN

WORDS AND

JACK

TEACHER IS AN

IL

iUS

100% MEEK

PICTURES BY
NOEL

BANANA
(FOR SCALE)

#LEARNING

☺ WELCOME TO ☺

BELTON PRIMARY

ESTABLISHED 1845

"Seeking Perfection Every Day"

HEADTEACHER: MR D. HOOPER

HULA HOOP ON THE ROOF

SEAGULL

BIG BELL

ASSEMBLY HALL

FLAG

BELTON PRIMARY

TREE

ENTRANCE

YO-YO ZONE

SCOOTER PARK

BELTON PRIMARY CLASSES

1. SQUIRREL CLASS
2. DARUDE CLASS
3. SQUID CLASS
4. FALAFEL CLASS
5. MINIDISC CLASS
6. CRABS CLASS
7. WEETABIX CLASS
8. ACORN CLASS

WELCOME TO BELTON PRIMARY

GIANT NUMBER ONE (NOT THAT KIND)

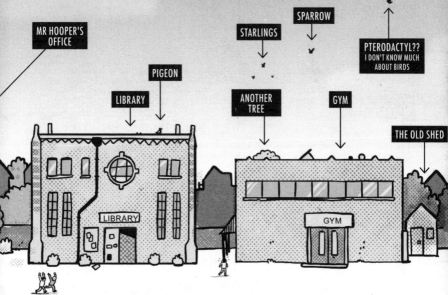

MR HOOPER'S OFFICE

SPARROW

STARLINGS

PTERODACTYL?? I DON'T KNOW MUCH ABOUT BIRDS

PIGEON

LIBRARY

ANOTHER TREE

GYM

THE OLD SHED

LIBRARY

GYM

I live in the town of Belton, and this is my school, Belton Primary. The school is Victorian, as in Queen Victoria, although I don't think she had anything to do with the actual building work.

HRH **QUEEN VICTORIA** 1819–1901 • REIGN: 63 YEARS BUILDINGS BUILT: NONE

13

HOME
& DRY!
Now do it
all again

TG Games
WALK the BLOCK

STRICTLY ONE PLAYER

Belton isn't really the kind of place that kings and queens visit much. There's Kings of Konvenience, the corner shop that is run by June King's mum and dad, but that's about it. And June normally comes to school on a scooter wearing a bright orange helmet and never in a solid gold carriage with a crown, so she's hardly the stuff of royalty.

ME
AGE: 10 • FRIENDS: 0

This is me. I tend to spend my break times playing "Walk the Block". It's a pretty simple one-player game. It's basically just me doing laps of the playground until the end of break. My highest score is 17 laps with only three instances of eye contact (four, if you include pigeons).

It's not that I don't want to do other things with my break times, like playing cat's cradle, or tossing round jokes or Frisbees, or sharing sweets or secrets or

EMPTY
BENCH
But for how
much longer?

14

PIGEON!
Awkward!

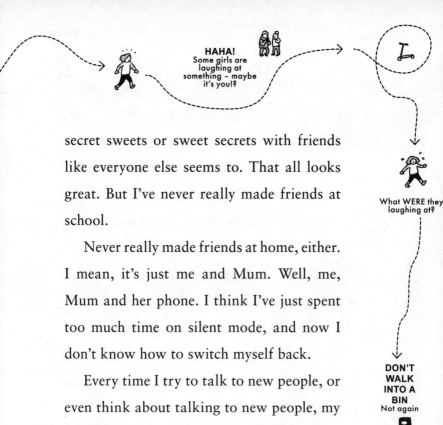
HAHA!
Some girls are laughing at something – maybe it's you!?

What WERE they laughing at?

DON'T WALK INTO A BIN
Not again

secret sweets or sweet secrets with friends like everyone else seems to. That all looks great. But I've never really made friends at school.

Never really made friends at home, either. I mean, it's just me and Mum. Well, me, Mum and her phone. I think I've just spent too much time on silent mode, and now I don't know how to switch myself back.

Every time I try to talk to new people, or even think about talking to new people, my words don't come out in order the proper. I have tried, but it never seems to go to plan. I wish I had a cool head, but my head is … stupid. That, and now about 18% metal.

At least being shy gives me a sneaky peek at what everyone else is up to in the playground. I like watching the world: you learn a lot that way. I can tell you who everyone is (from a distance, obvs) as I Walk the Block.

Just a tree, stay calm

BFFs!
Steer clear!

HALF WAY
There's no going back now

MR WARD
AGE: ?? (OLD)
TEAS:: 12

First is Mr Ward. He's our class teacher, which is nice because he's nice. He's the kind of teacher who would never shout at an old lady or make you do PE in your pants or make an old lady do PE in her pants. With Mr Ward, everything is big (hands, beard, heart).

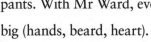

Next are the Surf Radicals. They're into surfing big time – online, mainly. That's where they came across parkour, which is French for "clambering about". The videos show people jumping from building to building like Spider-Man. These guys aren't at that level. That's Nucky, hopping off a curb and shouting "PARKOUR!" It's supposed to be an extreme sport. To me it seems extremely useless, but who knows – maybe one day we'll say, "Thank heavens for parkour!" (Probs not.)

The Surf Radicals

NUCKY
AGE: 11
FOLLOWERS: 16

That music is coming from those guys playing Frisbee. I call them the Hoody Gang. They're not a motorbikes-tattoos-swear words kind of gang; they're nice people. It's just that THEY ♥ HOODIES and wear them all the time. The one throwing the Frisbee is Sam Rowse. He likes hoodies so much sometimes he wears two, at once! Despite all the layers, he's pretty cool, I have to admit.

The Hoody Gang

SAM
AGE: 11
HOODIES: 12

These guys I call the String Kings, because they're always playing cat's cradle. Those two there are June and Adele. Cat's cradle is basically just tying knots but with more rules. June is the best at it. She can do a double corkscrew grandfather clock with sound effects.

String Kings

JUNE
AGE: 10
RUBBER BANDS: 23

ADELE
AGE: 10
IQ: 145

Loser Club

17

ME

June gets to practise her cat's cradle with all the elastic bands in her parents' corner shop. (It's not actually on the corner; it's on a straight bit of road. But the straight shop sounds weird.) Anyway, the most important bit about the shop is that it sells sweets, and when they go past their sell-by date, June brings them in. It happens about once a month on what we call Chew Chew Tuesdays. Those days are the best.

CHEW CHEW TUESDAYS
TYPICAL OFFERINGS

KITKAT CHUNKS
(HAVE A BREAK, THEY SAID...)

M&M&MS
(THE EXTRA M IS FOR MOULD)

DUMBIES
(SMARTIES THAT HAVE GONE PAST THEIR SELL-BY-DATE)

Adele is June's BFF. She's not just a String King. She's also Belton's IT girl. She's amazing with computers. She's read every issue of *PC Gone Mad* magazine, and she always wears a black polo neck like her hero, Steve Jobs, the inventor of Apples (computers). (Apples the fruit were invented by Sir Isaac Newton.) Adele just gets physics and science and all that stuff.

What else might you want to know about Belton Primary? The school used to be very important and fancy, but it's a bit-run down now. We're

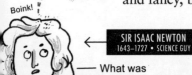
Boink!

SIR ISAAC NEWTON
1643–1727 • SCIENCE GUY

18

What was that?

always low on money, apparently. The Falafel class have only got eight pencils between them. Our poor, once glorious school—

PONK! ← WHAT THE WALNUT?!

Ow! What was that?! Something just hit me on the back of the head. Was it … a karate chop? I rub my head and turn around, slowly.

There's nobody there. It could have been a super-fast ninja, I guess? Then I notice a face grinning up at me from the ground. It's a cartoon smiley on a bright-red Frisbee, but I still feel the fickle tickle of embarrassment as I make eye contact with it. What's wrong with me?

"Hey, Braces!" says the Frisbee.

Is it … a magic, talking Frisbee?

"Over here!" says the Frisbee.

Oh no, wait – the voice is coming from across the playground. It's coming from … Sam. Sam Rowse!

GIANT NUMBER TWO
(NOT THAT KIND)

2 RETURN OF THE FRISBEE

Samuel Rowse, from the Hoody Gang. THE Sam Rowse. He's waving … he's waving at me! Behind him his whole gang are watching. I freeze in panic. It was bad enough when I thought a Frisbee was looking at me.

"The Frisbee!" says Sam. "Send it over!"

They want me to throw it back to them. Me!

I pick up the disc. I'm nervous. I'm not up to this. Sam and his friends are on the far side of the playground – about eleven million miles away.

"OK," I tell them, but so quietly, it may just be a thought. Other thoughts waddle through my brain, like, *What do I do now?* and *PEANUTS!* And *What the PEANUTS do I do now?*

hold the book down with your left hand here

"Throw the Frisbee, Braces!" another deeply unhelpful voice chips in. More people are watching now.

I try to wave at the gang, but as I am holding the Frisbee, it turns into a kind of wafting motion, like I am trying to shoo away a fart. Redness spreads across my cheeks like Ribena on a white carpet.

I have to return the Frisbee. It's simple! A single toss. Couldn't be simpler. But now even more people are watching. Not just Sam and the rest of the Hoody Gang, but Mr Ward has taken notice too, and Nucky and Adele and June, and basically everyone. The unblinking eyes of the Frisbee stare up at me.

I take a deep breath, step backwards and make the gentle back-and-forth motions of a professional Frisbee-ist. I imagine the sweet arc of my cross-playground toss back to Sam, as perfect as a rainbow. The kind of throw that will be sure to elicit cheers and back-slaps for years to come.

This is my moment. My perfect moment to

FLIPPING FUN
Hold the page as shown here and on page 22 and flip it to see the Frisbee go back and forth!

right thumb
here

21

hatch from the ugly duck egg of shyness and become a superb self-confident swan. All I have to do is throw the Frisbee.

But I don't let it go. Four, five, six times the Frisbee goes back and forth in my right hand. Then again and again, endlessly back and forth like a gif.

I see the mocking grin of the Frisbee, still firmly gripped by my own stupid, treacherous fingers. All around me people are pretending to look elsewhere, embarrassed on my behalf.

Let it go, I tell myself. *Let it go.* I can throw a Frisbee. I've done it a thousand times. I just have to Let. It. Go.

Sam is jogging over now. He will see how red I am, as red as a grilled tomato.

I have to do it now. I have to throw the Frisbee.

I'll count myself down: 3 ... 2 ... 1...

HOOOOOOOOOOOOOONK!

What the?!

The sudden noise surprises me so much that I finally let the Frisbee go.

right index
finger
here

Oop!

Fling!

I can only watch as the red disc rips through the air. It flies over Sam's head and then onwards and upwards – mostly upwards. The whole school watches in silence as it climbs up into the sky and then smashes straight into a window of the library block.

CRASH!

tinkle tinkle

"My Frisbee!" says Sam quietly, staring up at the black hole where a window used to be.

That couldn't have gone worse. Ugh! I wish someone would toss ME through a mysterious black hole, never to return.

HOOOOOOOOOOOOONK!

That noise again.

What is it?

The school gates swing open and a blacked-out stretch limo drives past the playground and into the car park. What the walnut is that all about?

3 MEET THE ACORNS

As we file into our classroom Mr Ward does the official class handshake with everyone.

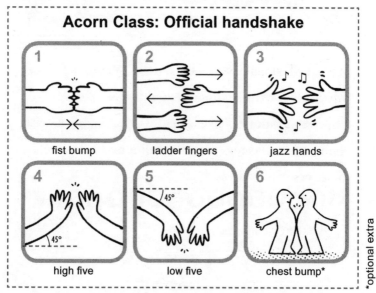

Acorn Class: Official handshake

1. fist bump
2. ladder fingers
3. jazz hands
4. high five
5. low five
6. chest bump*

*optional extra

Mr Ward named us the Acorns because he likes the way the tiny nuts, IRL, can grow into big, strong oak trees. I don't know if I'll ever grow into a big, strong oak of a person, but I quite fancy the beginning bit when you get buried deep in the cool, dark earth.

On the first day of term, Mr Ward made a big poster of an oak tree and we all put our fingerprints on it to make the leaves.

I like my seat because it's at the back. The nearest person to me is Hammy Potter, and he's locked in a cage. It's fine, though, because he's a rodent. Hammy is our class hamster and his full name is actually Hamilton Ariana McDonalds McHamface Yas-Queen Potter (the whole class named him together!). So technically he's H.A.M.M.Y. Potter. We normally just call him Hammy, though, to keep him grounded. We love Hammy.

WE ♥ HAMMY

NOM!

H.A.M.M.Y. POTTER
AGE: 1½
LIKES: PUMPKIN SEEDS,
ARIANA GRANDE

In class we learn about all sorts of things. Sometimes I think Mr Ward just looks out of the window and makes up this teaching thing as he goes along. In the past we've done things like pigeons

or chimneys. We once spent a whole term doing a special project about George, the window cleaner. Today we are learning about outer space.

I take my seat and get out my science exercise book.

Well, we're supposed to be learning about space... But before everyone has even finished sitting down, Nucky has his hand up. "Mr Ward," he calls out. "Who was in that limo?"

"I ... I don't know," Mr Ward says.

Several more hands are up in the air now. "None of these questions are about space, are they?" says Mr Ward.

"Why have they come here?" says Adele. "Is it a tech-millionaire looking to adopt?"

"Is it a Hollywood director looking for their next big star?" says Leona, fluttering her eyelashes and primping her hair.

There are so many hot takes on who it could be.

"Is it a Hollywood legend?"

"Is it a fancy European ruler?"

"Is it a fancy European pencil sharpener?"

"All right, all right!" says Mr Ward, holding his hands up. "Enough guesses! Stop! I'm sure Mr Hooper will tell us all in time. It will be good news, I'm sure."

It probably will be fine. What's that saying – when life gives you limos, make … limonade?

Everyone is quiet for a moment.

"Maybe Tim Holmes has come back!" says Sean. (One time Tim Holmes, who presents the weather on the local news, came to do the school raffle.)

27

"Please!" says Mr Ward. "Let's get back to space." He claps his hands together like a pair of meat cymbals. "I can see Tom has her science book out already. Tom, can you tell us all what we were looking at last time?"

Oh, crumbs. I wasn't expecting that! Limelight. Attention. I know what's next: the panic, the hot tomato face.

An un-ignorable silence sits in the air like a fart in a taxi.

Flippin' heck, that stinks!

Somebody open a window, please!

Oh, freaking pecan.

I look up at Mr Ward's beardy, expectant face. The whole class are watching me too. Twenty-four more faces, beardless this time. I feel dizzy. My forehead is on fire. My tummy is a bubbling cauldron. "I ... I..." The room is spinning like a Frisbee. There's never a freak weather event when you want one, is there?

BUT THEN—

RUMBLE! FREAK WEATHER EVENT??

A thunderous sound shakes the air above us. The whole class looks up to see a speaker, mounted high on the wall. It's a white plastic box with a glowing red light at the top, like a lunchbox that's turned evil.

It's especially surprising, as we don't even have a school intercom. It must be new.

"How do you do, er … young, er … people?"

The lunchbox / PA system has a gruff, low voice. No one here knows WHAT is going on. Mr Ward is frowning.

"Official Belton Primary announcement zero-zero-zero-zero-zero-zero-zero-zero-zero-one," says the box. In the pause we can hear the same message echoing around the school – there must be speakers in every room. "ITEM NUMBER ONE is … we 'ave a new intercom system."

We groan.

29

"Well, OBVIOUSLY!" shouts Gary Walters.

"ITEM TWO is a message for Neil in Acorn Class, from his mother. It says 'Neily-babes, please do not worry about your itchy patch. I have found a new cream we can try tonight, after your bath.'"

Neil groans and sinks into his chair as everyone around him tries to stifle their giggles.

"ITEM THREE is the headline news," says the voice. "This is the big one..." The voice is more excited now. We lean forward. "BOYS AND GIRLS of Belton Primary, please come to the main hall for a Very Important Assembly. The start time is in exactly five minutes. Attendance is compulsory. See you then. Over." And then there is the loud *cla-clunk* of a microphone turning off.

4 A NEW ARRIVAL

We are in the assembly hall, waiting. Kids in the middle, cross-legged, teachers round the side, cross-faced. We're all confused.

Then: the room goes dark. Spotlights swing around the gloom like dizzy bees. The deep voice from earlier blares out of speakers: "YOUNG PEOPLE OF BELTON, ARE. YOU. READY?!"

"Yes!" everyone cries. This is so exciting.

The door at the side of the stage swings open and a dry-ice fog fills the stage area. It has to be a celebrity! Somebody throws a pair of pants onto the stage in excitement. (Probably Lee Heritage – somehow he's convinced himself it's going to be Queen Victoria.)

A mysterious figure emerges from the smoke, their hands high in the air like they've just won Britain's Got Talent.

"IT'S THE INCREDIBLE, THE AMAZING, THE ABSOLUTELY PILLAGING ... MS FORTUUUUUUUNE!!"

THWUNK A spotlight rips through the darkness. Now we can see the person on stage in full. It's a woman. She is wearing a skirt suit, a smiley-face badge and has her hair in a tight bun that makes it look like she has an onion balanced on top of her head.

Ms Fortune looks out at us all, smiling. Her teeth twinkle in the lights like diamanté. Her eyebrows are two arches. Maybe it's the high heels, maybe it's the high bun, but she's definitely got something: Big Deal Energy. She is glamorous, she is cool, she is ... lost? I mean, she must be. What can someone like that be doing in a crummy place of learning like this?

Still, I can feel the excitement in the room. It's not often we have so many theatrics in the assembly hall. Most weeks we're lucky to get Mr Butler on piano, and the closest thing we get to Hollywood-style spotlights is the light bouncing off his bald head. This is like Tim Holmes coming to see us all over again – TIMES TEN.

MS FORTUNE
(OBVIOUSLY)

Ms Fortune stands at the front of the stage and smiles out at us. "Good afternoon, wonderful children of Belton!" she calls out.

All of a sudden, music starts to play from the speakers up on the walls. It's a jaunty upbeat tune like an old person's ringtone, a bit like "Supercalifragilisticexpialidocious", from the old *Mary Poppins*.

"I'm SO HAPPY to be here!" says Ms Fortune. She starts clapping above her head. Every single one of us immediately joins in. Kids are obedient like that, and besides, it's a good tune!

It's like a pop concert and everyone is LOVING IT, students and teachers alike. Mr Ships is beaming.

TAMBOURINE!

Mr Butler is clapping. Ms Burgess is cheering. Ms Patel is poking the air with a giant foam finger.

And then Ms Fortune starts SINGING. Singing!

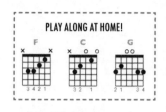

Hello, girls, and hello, boys,
Can't wait to get to know you,
My name, oh! It's Ms Fortune,
I've got great things to show you.
I'll build up your abilities, for exams and for tests,
I'll build you new facilities, bring extra-special guests,
Mould open, nurtured, educated youth.
Your grades will go right through the roof.
I'm for you, I'm for you, I'm Fortu-u-une!

"Everybody!" she cries.

"She's for uuus, she's for us, she's FORTUUUUUUNE!" the whole of Belton Primary sings back to her. Then there's more applause. Boy, are our hands going to be sore tomorrow.

There are going to be some sore cheeks too (face cheeks, I mean). Everyone is beaming big, broad smiles.

Or at least, almost everyone. Mr Ward has a face like thunder: his eyebrows are jagging downwards like two bolts of lightning. He looks … suspicious. And thinking about it, I guess he has a point. I mean, who is she? Some woman we've never met before. What about "Stranger Danger"? But then … the song! It's so catchy! It reminds us all of the old Mary Poppins movie, and that reminds us of the *new* Mary Poppins movie.

"Aha, thank you, thank you!" Ms Fortune laughs as the music fades out. "That was wonderful. What a great reception! I'm so glad you're as happy as I am to have me here. To have me here as … your new headteacher."

For a moment, there is silence.

Our new headteacher? What?? Then there's a GASP from everyone. And then a YAAAAY (from just the kids).

5 A WHOLE NEW HEAD

O ur new headteacher? What the walnut? I look over at Mr Ward. His mouth is a capital O with shock. All the teachers are the same. They look like the "surprised" section of an emoji keyboard. Mr Butler is frowning. Ms Patel is scrunching up her nose like a hamster. Ms Burgess is biting her nails.

The kids, meanwhile, are enthusiastically talking among themselves.

"Aha! I know, I know!" Miss Fortune says. "I can tell you're very excited. Well, I'm excited too! I've got big plans for this place. BIG plans!"

Everyone starts clapping again until Mr Ward stands up. "What about Dave?" he shouts across the hall. "What, pray, have you done with him?"

Who's Dave?

Mr Hooper
Headteacher

"Are you talking about Dave Hooper?" Ms Fortune asks.

Oh yeah, Mr Hooper! Our actual headteacher. Good point!

"Dave Hooper, yes! Mr Hooper," says Mr Ward. "He wouldn't just leave us!"

"Well ... he has," says Ms Fortune, steepling her fingers. "He's retired to, er... He's moved to a farm. In Spain. I'm glad you reminded me because he left a note for me to read to you all." Ms Fortune pulls a folded piece of paper from her jacket pocket. "'Dear students, colleagues, friends,' he says. 'I'm retiring and moving to a farm in Spain. So long and thanks for all the good memories. Please don't try and contact me because my phone doesn't work in Spain. Just to be clear, I'm in Spain. Yours sincerely, Señor Hooper, ex-headteacher of Belton Primary.'" Ms Fortune folds the paper and puts it back in her pocket. "So, as I was saying, I have big plans—"

"Retiring?" splutters Mr Ward, still standing. "Spain? But ... but ... he didn't say anything. I went to his birthday barbecue last month. He made his own burgers. We were going to go to a car boot sale together this weekend."

IS THAT ... A WHOPPER?

"Maybe it was a farewell barbecue?" Ms Fortune says.

"But ... but ... but his Volvo's outside!" wails Mr Ward, getting a bit desperate now.

"Is it? Oh, yes I remember … he went by helicopter. It landed on the gym-block roof at night-time.

"Oh, and I just saw another bit of the message," she adds, pulling the paper back out of her pocket. "He also says, 'Please don't ask questions about all of this; that is my parting wish.' So there you go. You heard the man. No further questions! That's what he wanted. Let's all say a big thank you and a safe helicopter flight to Mr Hooper."

"Thank you, Mr Hooper," the whole hall of kids says in sing-song unison, without even thinking. I do it too, I can't help it – schoolkids are well-trained like that.

"Thank you, Dave," Mr Ward says, quietly, before sinking back down into his chair. And then, quieter still, he adds, *"Adiós."*

It's not really like Mr— Sorry, I mean *Señor* Hooper, to just go off like that. I don't remember ever seeing him in a helicopter. It's a shame: he was nice to us. He even always brought Hammy Potter some pumpkin seeds for his birthday (28 April – Hammy's a classic Taurus). I wonder if he'll still

Señor Hooper
He's Spanish now

wear the same green cardigan every day, even in Spain. I never really thought of him as a real person who does things like go to Spain. But then I never really thought he had a first name until Mr Ward just started banging on about it, so who knows?

"Thank you for your question anyway, Mister...?" says Ms Fortune.

"Mr Ward," says Mr Ward.

"Lovely. Well, thank you, Mr Wart."

"Ward!" says Mr Ward. But Ms Fortune has moved on.

"So, as you heard in my song," she says, "I have big plans. And I'll need some help to carry them out, so I want you to meet my assistants. Well, I say my assistants. Really they're your caretakers. They are going to TAKE CARE of you."

"Yeah!" shouts someone. "Whoop!" says someone else. They're just caretakers! We really will cheer anything at this point.

Ms Fortune gestures to the side of the stage. "Here they are: my friends, your facility managers. They are Chip Pin and Serge Price!"

Two men walk out onto the stage. One is shortish and kind of big. The other is tallish and lean. The first

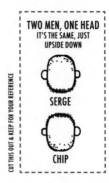

has a shaved head with a tufty beard and the second has a shaved face with tufty hair, so it kind of looks like they both have the same head, just upside down. They are wearing identical navy blue v-neck jumpers which don't fit either of them. They are both wearing smiley-face buttons, just like Ms Fortune. They stand either side of Ms Fortune and wave.

42

SERGE PRICE
HAIR: NONE • BEARD: SOME
BODY SHAPE: PEAR

CHIP PIN
HAIR: SOME • BEARD: NONE
BODY SHAPE: LEEK

"Hello, I am Mr Pin," says the one with hair.

"An' I'm Mr Price," says the other one.

"And that's not all!" says Ms Fortune. "These are your new teachers." Six people step out onto the stage. "Hello, I'm Mr Derry," says the first man, smiling out at us.

"And I'm Miss Ferry," says the next person.

One by one they introduce themselves. They're VERY smiley.

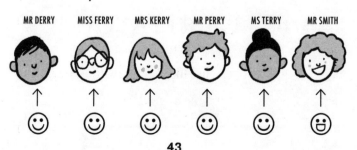

MR DERRY   MISS FERRY   MRS KERRY   MR PERRY   MS TERRY   MR SMITH

"But the kids already have teachers," shouts Mr Ward. "Us!" A couple of the other teachers join in: "Yeah!", "Good point!" and "What about us?"

"I'm glad you asked!" says Ms Fortune. "It's your lucky day. All current teachers are entitled to a very special offer. It's the Scholars' Corporate Retirement Asset Package Scheme – SCRAPS!"

"Retirement?" says Mr Rowlands. "But I'm only twenty-sev—"

Ms Fortune talks over him. "It's quite the offering!" she says.

"But teaching is our calling," Mr Butler says. "It's wonderful! We can't just give it up."

"I always say, teaching is a work of HEART," says Ms Patel. "Our students need us. And we need them!"

"Very good," says Ms Fortune. "I admire your dedication. Really, I do. Well done. But I should say that anyone who leaves today will get …

A BIG CASH PAYOUT!"

She produces a wad of extra-large novelty cheques from the edge of the stage. They're great, wobbly sheets of card as big as lilos.

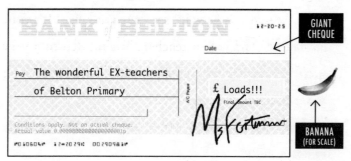

Suddenly the teachers aren't quite so keen to stay. "Well, er..." a couple of them say. "I suppose we could find another calling." And as one, they head up to the stage, ready to take their cheques. "Thanks, Ms Fortune," they say and then, "BYE, KIDS!" as they file straight out of the hall. "So long!"

From out in the corridor, we can hear high fives and stifled shrieks of joy. I'm pretty sure I can hear the pop of champagne corks. A muffled cheer. Doors swung open, slammed shut. Then the screeching of tyres on tarmac as ten teachers' cars take off at once.

SQUEAL

H O N K

HONK

H O N K

H

They said teaching was a calling, but I guess the money called louder. *Ring ring kerching.*

Ms Fortune turns her attention back to us, the kids. "So," she says. "All your lovely teachers have left you."

"Ha-HUMM," says Mr Ward, clearing his throat as quietly as you might fire a cannon. "Not ALL the teachers."

Good old Mr Ward! When money called, he was on flight mode.

Ms Fortune drops her head to the side like a curious velociraptor. "Er ... well, no. Not all the teachers. You stuck around, didn't you? Well done, you. Well done, Mr Wart."

"Mr WARD!" says Mr Ward. "I literally just told you!"

"I'm so glad you'll be staying," she continues. She gives him some serious side-eye and her mouth tightens into a very thin line. "I'm sure we're going to get along—" she looks straight at him—"like a house on fire."

Then she turns back to the rest of us, her smile full beam again. "This is going to be a wonderful time for every one of us. Very rewarding, I would say. A bold new era for Belton Luxcorp Academy of Student Teaching. That's the school's new name, by the way. But why take my word for how great a headteacher I am?! Let's hear from some of my previous students who have all gone on to be very successful..." The lights dim and a series of short video clips plays on the screen behind Ms Fortune.

"Right stop that," says Ms Fortune quickly. "So you see that I really am a wonderful force for good! If you have any questions, why not read my book!"

THE #1 REGIONAL BESTSELLER

FORTUNE

MOULDING OPEN NURTURED & EDUCATED YOUTH

As seen on screen!
A computer screen, one time

Signed by the author
's assistant

"THIS IS A ... BOOK" Guardian

Oooooooh, she's written a book? Well, she MUST be nice. Everyone who writes a book is an absolute solid gold legend.

"Well, that's it," says Ms Fortune. "But before you go, I've got something for all of you too. When you leave, please don't forget your—"

"Goody bags!" all the new teachers shout in unison. From behind their backs, they produce a buttload of colourful paper bags.

"Stickers!" says Mr Derry.

"Bookmarks!" says Miss Ferry.

"A tiny box of raisins!" says Mrs Kerry.

"A rainbow rubber!" says Mr Smith.

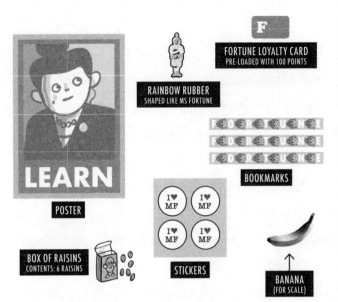

POSTER

LEARN

RAINBOW RUBBER
SHAPED LIKE MS FORTUNE

FORTUNE LOYALTY CARD
PRE-LOADED WITH 100 POINTS

BOOKMARKS

BOX OF RAISINS
CONTENTS: 6 RAISINS

STICKERS

I♥MF I♥MF
I♥MF I♥MF

BANANA
(FOR SCALE)

"OHMIGOSSSH!" screams June. (She loves a bookmark.) In fact, everyone is shrieking. Goody bags?! Arlo Sumac – a boy from the year below – stands up and then sits down immediately. This is getting too much.

Everyone feverishly rushes to the stage. They grab a bag each and run from the room, chomping raisins and sticking stickers and bookmarking books as they go.

And everyone is talking a mile a minute.

"Our head is AMAZING!"

"This is so great!"

49

✄ cut out and keep a FORTUNE bookmark of your very own!

"I'm going to get a tiny guitar!"

"And Mr Hooper? Mr Who?-per, more like."

Once most of the hall is clear, I shuffle up and take one of the last remaining goody bags. Yes, this is all a bit odd and yes, I am a bit suspicious about Ms Fortune ... but not enough to stop me enjoying a rainbow rubber.

Just as I get to the exit, I feel a tap on the shoulder.

It's Mr Pin. "Thomasina Ginger?" he says, frowning as he reads my name from his clipboard.

"Ye... Yes?"

He snatches the bag out of my hand and upturns it into a nearby bin. "Not for you. You need to come with me."

What the walnut?

BIG BIN

BANANA SKIN
(QUITE SLIPPY)

WASTE
WATCHER

BANANA
(FOR SCALE)

6 DING DONG

Sam and I are marched along the corridor by Mr Pin and Mr Price. It's too serious for me and Sam to chat but I'm fine with that. I'm not one for idle chit-chat. If I tried to shoot the breeze with someone I'd probably miss and shoot myself in the eye or something. And ESPECIALLY with Sam Rowse, king of the hoodies (my words). I don't know what to say to him at the best of times, and now it's pretty much the worst of times.

I keep my eyes down as we walk until the four of us get to the end of the corridor. There, instead of the normal door, is a lift, and it appears to be made out of GOLD. It's so fancy and new, you can practically hear the gleam. What the walnut?

Mr Pin presses a button and the the doors slide apart with a ding-dong. It is a lift – a solid gold flaming lift!

Sam catches my eye and raises his eyebrows in a way that seems to say "Sheesh!" and "This is weird" all at once.

Once we're inside the lift, a robotic voice says, "To proceed, please place a registered digit on the FSU."

Mr Price puts his index finger onto a little black panel. "Good morning, Mr Price," says the lift. "Please now enter the alpha-numeric access code." Mr Price taps out a password on a tiny keyboard.

"Thank you. Going up," says the lift again.

"A talking lift … with a fingerprint scanner thing and a secret access code. How much would that cost?" says Sam with his forehead.

"You have arrived at: the boardroom," says the lift.

"Right, you kids!" says Mr Price. "In you go!"

We step into the middle of what used to be Mr Hooper's office.

Back in Mr Hooper's day (yesterday!?) it was a pretty normal room with a desk, a computer and a jug of water with plastic cups for visiting kids. The walls were covered with student artwork.

But, now, well – look!

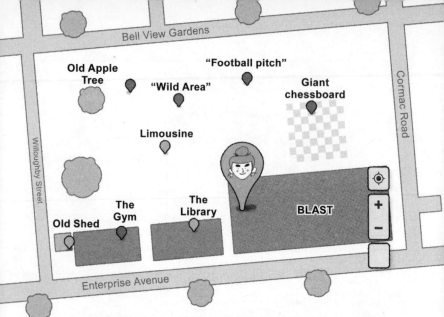

Ms Fortune is standing at the big window, looking out. From up here you can see the whole playground all at once, like a picture from Google Earth. You can see everything from up here.

Ms Fortune must be a gazillionaire, to drive a car like that. Why would a limo-driving gazillionaire want to be the headteacher of a crummy old school like this?

Mr Price stands behind us at the door. Mr Pin is sat at a table at the side. He's wearing a massive pair of headphones connected to a stack of old-fashioned metal boxes. He's frowning and making notes on a clipboard as he listens. Is he … a hipster?

Sam and I stand awkwardly in the middle of the room, waiting for someone to speak. Mr Price and Mr Pin are silent. Ms Fortune takes a last slurp from her cola can and drops it into the bin (the paper one!).

"Well?" she says finally. "What are you waiting for?"

What are we waiting for? Maybe we're supposed to order something. Should I have cola or cucumber water? I'll just get what Sam gets. He starts to shuffle towards a chair so I follow.

"I DIDN'T SAY SIT!" she shouts suddenly, smashing her fists into the desk. What the walnut!? "You kids... You little ... smashers. You broke my window, didn't you?"

She is close enough that I can see several thick hairs sticking out of the mole on her cheek, like a tarantula trying to escape a black hole. She looked so glamorous and cool from far away. But up close ... kind of gross. Like a mouldy Snickers.

"Think you're the Big Cheeses, do you? The Top Dogs?" she says. "Well, I'm watching you. The alphas. That's Step One when you arrive at any institution. A school. A Big City firm. A prison. They're all the same. You work out who the alphas are, and then you dominate them. You show them who's boss, then ... no more bad behaviour."

"We're not the big cheeses..." says Sam.

"I'm really not..." I say. "I'm the smallest possible cheese."

| TINY CHEDDAR | WEE BRIE | SINGLE GRAIN OF PARMESAN | ME |

But Ms Fortune ignores us. She turns to the window. "Children, hello!" she says. Somehow, her voice booms out of speakers around the playground below.

Everyone immediately stops what they are doing and looks up.

"Are you all enjoying your goody bags?" she asks, which is immediately met by a huge cheer from our fellow students.

"Well, I'm so pleased. And the next offering is even better: it's donuts! As many extra-special double-glazed fine-fill donuts as you can eat. So what do you think? Let me hear you go nuts for donuts!"

There is more cheering.

"But sadly, there are no-nuts. I should say that WAS to be the next offering ... but now it's cancelled. I'm very sorry but because of some bad, bad, bad children, it won't be possible to give these out today."

"Boo!" the children shout.

"I know, I know. Such a shame!" says Ms Fortune. "But don't blame me, blame Thomasina Ginger and Sam Rowse. This morning these two mindless vandals broke a window and the donuts will have to be returned to pay for it to be replaced. You'll understand, I'm sure. Glazing is expensive."

"What?" says Sam. "That's not fair... We didn't... They're going to hate us."

"OK, that's it," says Ms Fortune, shooing us away. "Mr Pin, Mr Price – take them down. I've got important headteacher business to get on with." She sits down at her computer. It's one of those big fancy ones with a giant flat monitor. I can see the glowing screen reflected in the window behind her. It

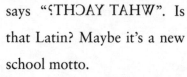 says "STHƆAY TAHW". Is that Latin? Maybe it's a new school motto.

"This is so unfair!" says Sam again as we head back to our classroom. "It was an accident! It wasn't our fault!"

He doesn't say it was my fault, but maybe he should. It was me who threw the Frisbee.

I don't say anything.

"Now everyone's going to blame us."

Ms Fortune's not as nice as she makes out, I say. Sam doesn't respond. Probably because I don't say it aloud, just in my head. We carry on in silence. I can tell that he's worried, but what can I say that would help?

The classroom goes quiet when we push open the door. Then:

"Oh, it's them," says Tina.

"Don't be mean," whispers June, but nobody really hears her. They are all too busy giving us major stink-eyes.

"I love donuts," says Sean, looking at his empty hands as if he's holding invisible baked goods. "How could you!?"

ISSUE #1   "FREE"

The Belton Bugle

THE _NEW_ BELTON LUXCORP® ACADEMY OF STUDENT TEACHING™ NEWSLETTER

FORTUNE IS FANTASTIC

Belton Luxcorp Academy© of Student Teaching™ has a new head and opinion polls have her approval ratings at 99 per cent. Ms Fortune WOWED at her first ever assembly. "It was the best thing to ever happen to me," says one student. Other children were impressed with their new class teachers. "I don't even remember my old teacher's name!" said one. "I think it was Mr … Teachy?" added a third, unhelpfully.

CONTINUED ON PAGES 2, 3, 5 AND 12-17

NEW NEWSLETTER

We have a new newsletter, obviously.

SCHOOL TRIP

As a globally minded institution we of course wish to engage with the international community.

We are planning a special school trip for selected lucky students.

CONTINUED ON NEXT PAGE

SO LONG, OLD HEAD

Mr Hooper has moved to Spain. No further questions.

ADVERTORIAL

Luxberg Industries©®

They're a nice company

THE _NEW_ BELTON LUXCORP® ACADEMY OF STUDENT TEACHING™ NEWSLETTER

CONT FROM FRONT PAGE It will be to Paris, France, home of the "french stick". A chance to learn language, culture and much much more. To see the Mona Lisa, the Eiffel Tower and other French things like garlic and berets. Selections are to take place over the coming months. *Bonne chance* to everyone.

GYM BLOCK UPGRADE

That Gym Block has seen a lot of hula hoops, many bean bags and a load of balls. It has also seen better days. We are currently in consultation with local businesses to reinvigorate the hall.

PLANTS FOR ALL

We are very lucky to have new potted plants hanging throughout the school buildings. Plants have been said to reduce "bad vibes" by up to 50 per cent. They're good for mental health. And then there's the environment. Plants are an oasis for bees, wasps and flies. This will explain any buzzing sound and shouldn't be investigated any further. Also, doesn't it just go to show how Ms Fortune cares about all little lives? She's tremendous.

VOX POPS
THE VOICE OF THE PLAYGROUND

"It's all so exciting!"
Egg, year one

"What will be next?"
Yottam, year two

"Such a shame about that window."
Ava, year three

Q	P	P	R	I	V	A	T	I	S	A	T	I	O	N
C	C	T	A	R	E	C	Z	O	F	E	Q	S	A	Z
Q	J	C	O	R	P	O	R	A	T	E	F	E	U	Q
S	Y	N	E	R	G	Y	F	O	R	T	U	N	E	N
S	H	A	R	I	N	G	D	U	H	B	N	O	G	A
E	G	H	P	X	F	C	X	G	I	Q	N	S	O	V
T	A	R	P	R	O	F	I	T	E	E	R	I	N	G
B	G	K	O	Y	U	S	C	H	O	O	L	N	F	K

Wordsearch
Sun
School
Fun
Sharing
Fortune
Synergy

7

NEW ERA

Ms Fortune has been at Belton Primary for just a few days, but already it's so different! For one thing, it's not even called Belton Primary any more. It's Belton Luxcorp© Academy of Student Teaching™. There's a new flag and everything, right up by the old bell.

Everyone, apart from Sam and me, seems pretty happy to have a new headteacher. Ms Fortune has definitely zhuzhed up the place. The flaky cream corridors have been repainted and there are hanging plants everywhere. And she's even brought in a loyalty scheme with special cards and everything. It's supposed to "encourage behavioural excellence, respect and complicity". After what happened with the Frisbee, Sam and I both started out on -250 points.

But it's not just all that, it's the promises!

YOU MUST HAVE 75+ POINTS TO SIT HERE

YOU MUST HAVE 100+ POINTS TO USE THIS DOORWAY

QUILTED
200+ POINTS

STANDARD 2-PLY
50-200 POINTS

USED
LESS THAN 50 POINTS

Ms Fortune has promised SO MUCH. It's like how Christmas Eve is fun even though you don't have any presents yet. You have the promise of presents, and they could be ANYTHING. A Nintendo Switch, a book, a watch, a tub of slime... (And then on Christmas day: usually socks.)

For the kids of Belton Primary, Ms Fortune's promises are the presents under the tree, just waiting to be unwrapped.

I hear them talking excitedly as I play Walk the Block at lunchtime.

"I heard she's going to buy us a luxury new sports hall!"

"I heard she's going to get us all tiny golf carts to drive!"

"I heard we're going to get a Wii in the games room."

"I heard we're going to get a games room!"

"Everyone is so happy," Sam says to me. And that's the other thing that's changed. The donut incident was bad for me, but for Sam it was a catastrophe. Nobody wants to be associated with him any more. So he's been reduced to hanging out with me. Walk the Block: player two has entered the game.

Nobody wants to speak to either of us. We're outcasts. I'm used to being all alone at break times, but for Sam this is all new. He's having trouble adjusting.

"This is so unfair!" Sam says for the hundredth time. "Ms Fortune has turned everyone against us."

I try to nod, smile and shrug all at the same time but somehow my face gets tangled up and I look more like I'm having a brain freeze. Poor Sam ... having only me for company.

"Oh, look who it is," says Michael, one of the hoody gang, as we pass. "Sam and Tom. The mindless vandals that cost us all a lorry-load of donuts." The rest of the gang – Sam's old gang – all tut and turn away from us, pulling their hoods up as they do.

"You don't understand," says Sam. "She's not what she seems. She wants you to hate us! That window thing was an accident. We shouldn't be blamed like this!"

"You vandals should have thought of that before you broke Ms Fortune's trust," says another hoody member.

"And her window!" adds another.

"Well, hold up ... the Frisbee thing was an accident," June says quietly. "That could have been any of us."

"Huh! Not me!" says Tina, glaring at June. "I'm loyal – I've got, like, a thousand points to prove it."

The loyalty scheme wasn't even going back then, I think, but ... oh nuts, what's the use in arguing with these guys. They're never going to change their minds about me and Sam. June's taking a real risk standing up for us. She'd probably be an outcast too, if it weren't for the fact that she's clutching a shopping bag bulging with semi-perished sweets. It's a Chew Chew Tuesday. The worst possible day to be an outcast...

8 SWEET LIFE

Remember I told you that Chew Chew Tuesdays are when June brings in expired sweets from her parents' shop? They're the best days. Sometimes Gareth brings in spare samples from his parents' shop but sadly for him Carpet Tile Mondays have never really taken off.

Kids crowd around her – a real life candy crush. There's always a massive competition to get anything, but even I manage to get a sneaky treat sometimes. Not this week though.

Nobody wants to make space for me or Sam to get our hands on anything.

Sam sighs. I feel sorry for him. Normally, he's right at the centre of things. "Who's that?" he says, pointing to a woman walking from the gym block. She's smartly dressed in a suit and clip-cloppy shoes – definitely not a teacher. She's reading something on a Luxcorp© clipboard. In her other hand is a white paper cup. "What's she up to?"

"Just one pack of Mentos left!" calls June. "I think I'll take these!" she laughs.

"I want them!" says a first-year boy, jumping up.

"Me!" says another.

"No, me!"

The younger kids are chasing after June now. Everyone's laughing. There's a good atmosphere.

"So long, suckers!" says June, running away. She hasn't noticed the woman walking towards her.

"Look out!" says Sam, but it's too late. June bowls into her.

WHAM

"WHAT THE—!?" shrieks the woman as her drink flies up into the air and she's all over the ground. Mentos skitter scatter all around them.

"Oops!" says June, clambering to her feet. "Sorry about that."

The woman looks furious. Poor June! I hate confrontation of any kind, and the whole thing makes me wince. I clench my teeth together. And then, just for a moment, there is a crackling in my brain as if I've been eating popping candy.

"SWEETIES!" shrieks the woman. "Ghastly sweeties! No sweeties!" she shouts. And then, quieter, she repeats it. "No sweeties." She picks up a few of the Mentos.

"I'm really sorry," says June again.

The woman is muttering to herself. "Smoothies only. No sweeties." She sobs quietly into the six Mentos she's got in her hands. "Mustn't eat them. Mustn't..."

"Let me help you!" comes a voice. It's Ms Fortune, jogging out from the gym block.

"I am SO sorry," she says to the woman. "This is

not what it's like here, please don't worry. The kids are completely under control."

"Sweeties, though?" the woman says. "We can't have that. Fresh, organic smoothies only. Artisanal avocados, sure. Quinoa on sourdough. That kind of thing. Not sweeties!"

"Not sweeties, no! Of course not. And let me buy you a new smoothie," says Ms Fortune, picking up the dropped cup. "A staff member will be right out to finish your tour of the buildings."

Soon enough, Ms Terry jogs over and takes the woman by the arm, leading her away.

Ms Fortune rounds on the rest of us. "Who dared to bring sweets into the school?"

There's a shocked silence. This isn't the sparkly,

fun version of Ms Fortune that everyone is used too.

"It was me," June says, coming forward. "The sweets are from my parents' shop. I'm sorry, I really didn't mean to bump into—"

"Bump into!? *Bump!??!?* If only it were so gentle as a little bump, don't you think, everyone?" says Ms Fortune, turning to all the kids gathered around. "Sadly your fellow student June has been bringing in sweets and – much worse – interrupting important grown-up business. It really is a shame, because now we have to bring in new rules. I didn't want to do this, it's all June's fault."

"Boo!" call the kids.

"That nice lady was checking the school as a potential location for a music video with many famous pop stars in it. And there was going to be a Ferris wheel and dancers and fireworks. But now it's all cancelled, and it's all June's fault."

"But I didn't—" exclaims June, but her voice is drowned out by booing.

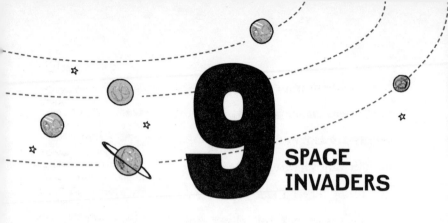

9 SPACE INVADERS

"**Y**our task for today," Mr Ward says after lunch, "is to come up with a fun way to remember the order of the planets." He writes MNEMONIC on the board. Is that ... a word?

"A mnemonic is a creative trick to help you remember things. The order of the planets, for instance. Mercury, Venus, Earth, Mars, Jupiter, Saturn, Uranus, Neptune. To remember that, we need memorable phrases using the first letters – M, V, E, M, J, S, U, N. For example," says Mr Ward "you could have My Very Excited Mum Just Served Us Noodles." I love noodles. Isn't it weird to think that teachers might eat them too? And have mothers?

Noodles!

Mum

72

"So that's mine – see if you can do better. You can work together, in twos or threes."

Oh nuts. I hate working in twos or threes. The pairing up process is the most painful popularity contest, and ol' Tom Ginger always comes out on bottom.

COOL MNEMONICS

To remember the order of the compass points (North East South West), think of "Never Eat Shredded Wheat".

To remember how to spell diarrhoea, take the first letters from "Dash In A Real Rush, Hurry Or Else Accident".

To remember how to spell MNEMONIC, take the first letters from "Memories Not Easily Made? Oh No! I'm Confused".

Everyone else immediately gets into their little groups. It's beautiful to watch, in a way. Like swooping starlings making shapes in the sky.

Each group sits at a table together. I'm left standing at the back, alone.

Although this time I'm not alone. There are two other abandoned birds.

SAM   JUNE

No one has spoken to June since lunchtime. Not everyone completely believes the pop-video thing, but everyone believes there was going to be something. And whatever it was, June ruined it. Even Adele has been avoiding her – she's gone in a group with Matt and Ben. But she keeps looking over at June. "Don't talk to her," Greg whispers.

73

"She's always been selfish!" says Matt.

"That's just not true!" hisses back Adele, frowning.

"Looks like it's us three," Sam says to me and June. Well, this is new. Me and Sam and June. June and Sam and me. Three amigos!

We sit down. The room is quiet, with everyone busy working in their twos and threes. Occasionally someone will glance over at us – the outcasts – but largely we're ignored. June barely speaks. She's so sad that a tear slips down her face. I clench my jaw in frustration – poor June doesn't deserve this kind of treatment -- and then … and this is weird, but … I can hear something … in my brain … voices. First it's Mr Price's voice: *"I'm on it, Ms Fortune,"* he says. *"Heading to the classroom right now."*

I look around, confused. There's no sign of Mr Price, but there was his voice in my head.

KRAK!

the classroom door bursts open.

It's Mr Price. Mr Pin is just behind him. They look angry.

They're here! I knew they would be, but ... how did I know?

"Hey!" says Mr Ward. "What is the meaning of this?"

"Spot check" says Mr Pin. "Just want to make sure everything here is ... in order." He picks up a pencil case from the nearest table and shakes the contents out onto the desk. Pens, pencils, a compass and a little ruler clatter out.

"Hey!" says Mr Ward, but Mr Pin carries on inspecting the room as if he doesn't hear him at all.

Mr Price is in front of the poster of the fingerprint oak tree. "You don't have me on here..." he says to Mr Ward, with a cruel smile. He turns and takes a bottle of black paint from the art shelf and splodges some into a palette.

"Mr Pin, please..." says Mr Ward, "don't ruin the children's artwork." But Mr Pin takes no notice. He puts his massive thumb into the thick paint puddle and then smooshes it, COVERED in paint, right into the middle of the tree. We are all too shocked to say anything.

"There you have it!" Mr Pin laughs, beaming a big mean smile at all of us.

"Hey, Mr Pin. Look at this!" says Mr Price. "It's a rat. Come and look." Oh no, not Hammy Potter!

10

HAMSTER... DAMN

Mr Price brings his eye down to the level of the Hammy's cage, like the T-Rex in *Jurassic Park*. Hammy is frozen in fear. "Is it a rat ... or what??"

Hammy's sweet little nose twitches nervously as Mr Price reaches through the hatch at the top of the cage and picks him up by the scruff of his sweet little neck. He squeaks helplessly. A chorus of stifled cries comes from the kids.

"Hello, little one," says Mr Price.

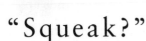

"Squeak?"

says Hammy. His body is shot through with tension, there is fear in his little beady eyes. The whole class is silent as we watch this cruel oaf man-handling our furry friend.

Mr Price prods him in the belly. "He is fat."

It's almost too much to bear. I want to say something ... but I can't make myself. I'm not the only one. A tense silence hangs in the air. And a hamster.

"That's Hammy Potter," says Mr Ward. "He's our class hamster. Please release him."

Mr Price gives him another prod.

"Just stop!" says Mr Ward.

Nucky stands up. "He's our hamster. His favourite music is Ariana Grande and his favourite seed is pumpkin."

Adele stands up too. "We all look after him."

"WE ALL LOVE HIM," adds Nucky, gesturing to the WE ♥ HAMMY display.

Mr Pin pokes Hammy in the cheek with his painty finger. Black splodges in the shape of an exclamation mark stick to his fur.

"Don't be rough with him," says Nucky. "When hamsters are scared, they are unpredictable. If they're really frightened they can poo themselves."

"Don't be silly," says Mr Price. "He likes it!"

And then—

* ♫ ♪ ♬ !!! *

THE HIGH-PITCHED TINY SQUELCH OF A HAMSTER BUMHOLE

"EUUURGH!"

Mr Price drops Hammy and tiny brown coco poops spray everywhere. Hammy falls to the table, and then to a chair, and then the floor.

Squeak! Bounce! Squeak, squeak! Bounce.

He tumbles across the floor. Then he finds his tiny feet, and he's scurrying away. "OI!" shouts Mr Pin, stamping his feet – but Hammy is away. He is a blur of orange and white heading for the wall, and he's gone.

"He pooed on me!" shouts Mr Price. "That little RAT!"

Everyone ignores him. "Where's Hammy?" Nucky shouts.

"He went down there."

"Behind the drawers!"

More people join the search, but it's a lost cause. The ragged old skirting board has more holes than a colander.

"He's gone," Nucky says.

Hammy?

Hammy?

Hammy?

11

LOST

Mr Price and Mr Pin have left us at last. The whole class is going mad, searching for Hammy. Nobody minds that Sam and June are helping too. Sam is on his hands and knees trying to peer under the skirting board. Mr Ward helped June move the drawers away from the wall. Adele is doing something with a little pail. Nucky is looking a little pale. He's clambered up a bookcase, in case an aerial view helps.

I'm in my seat by Hammy's empty cage. I don't know how to help. I'm too upset. This is horrible. Poor Hammy! I can't believe he's gone. And all because those bullies Mr Pin and Mr Price bowled into our classroom and terrified him. They shouldn't have done that. He's, like, a fiftieth of their size! I'm so—

"*Well done, Mr Pin and Mr Price.*" A voice in my head cuts me off mid-thought. It's Ms Fortune. And I realize I've clenched my teeth again. "*That'll keep them in check.*"

I unclench my teeth. What the walnut just happened?

I clench my teeth together again and I can hear Mr Pin and Mr Price laughing. "*We're coming back up now,*" says one of them. I unclench and then I hear nothing.

I clench again and I can hear Ms Fortune, Mr Pin and Mr Price as clear and loud as if they were right beside me. It's

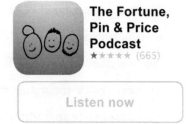

The Fortune, Pin & Price Podcast
★★★★★ (665)

Listen now

like I'm wearing invisible earbuds and they're on a Podcast. I can hear them all ... somehow.

"*... had to buy her a completely new smoothie ...*" Ms Fortune.

UNCLENCH This is weird.

CLENCH "*... no, Chip, smoothies! I'm talking about MONEY! I'm all about it ... and I need MORE. The spa is just stage one.*"

UNCLENCH Mr Ward's voice this time. "Well, I … I don't know what to say," he says. I blink and realize that he is actually in the room with me. He pulls off his glasses and wipes his eye. "I guess … we should just go back to the planets. Leave those seeds on the floor there. Let's hope Hammy's doesn't d— Er, well, let's hope he comes back soon." He seems shaken up.

Everyone goes back to their places. Except for Nucky, who is now working his way along the back wall, tapping away in desperation for a hidden nook (and/or cranny) that could be hiding Hammy.

Adele puts the finishing touches to her hamster trap. Hopefully that will work!

PUMPKIN SEEDS
PAPER TOWEL
BUCKET
TINY LADDER

FREE!
HAMSTER FOOD
this way

LIGHT UP BILLBOARD (TYPICAL ADELE)

I'm back in my seat. I can't think about the planets – I'm too busy thinking about what on earth is going on with my jaw and the voices in my mind. Am I a mind-reading mentalist? A psychic? How? Why? *Whu?*

12 OWN GOAL

Thunk thunk thunkity thunk. That's the sound of a hundred netballs pounding into the shiny wooden floor of the gym block. It's music, in a way. Thunky music.

We're wearing plimsolls, shorts and white t-shirts, as is the Official Belton Primary PE kit. Mr Ward is wearing the same brown suit he always wears, but he also has sweatbands on his wrists and a stopwatch round his neck.

The t-shirts are supposed to be plain but I never seem to have one. Today I've had to wear one of Mum's old ones that says FINGER OF FUN – GAMER CONFERENCE '05 on the back. (PE = Physical Education. But also, in so many ways, PE = Pure Embarrassment.)

STOCK STILL

Today is netball, which means at least I get a bib to cover my t-shirt. The bib is green, smells of blue cheese and has big white letters on it – GD, Goal Defence. But right now, all the action is at the other end. Which is good.

I'm more comfortable away from the action. There's been a lot going on recently and I've not had much chance to process it because I've suddenly got people to hang out with: Sam and June – my fellow rejects. It's nice, for me at least.

I haven't told them I've started hearing voices in my head though. We're friends, but not quite at the BTW-I-might-be-psychic level just y— THUNK!

Ow! A netball bounces off my head. The action is now down this end of the pitch.

The netball pings off my head and into the net. The very net I'm supposed to be defending. Oh, nuts. My head just scored an own goal.

But then, suddenly, the ball stops. Pausing in mid-air, like a glitch.

PSSSSSSSSST goes the ball, still stuck. It's been punctured by a spiky stick. PSSST it continues, like a shish kebab with a secret.

At the other end of the stick is Mr Price. He is wearing a yellow hard hat, like a builder. He doesn't even notice everyone yelling at him ("Hey!" "Boo!" "OI!" etc). He just calmly brings the flaccid rubber ex-ball down and scrapes it off into an industrial bin bag that Mr Pin holds open.

"WHAT ARE YOU DOING?" shouts Mr Ward.

"That's our ball!" shouts Sandra. "We need it!"

"The gym block..." starts Mr Price, looking up. Thunk thunk thunk – another netball is slowly bouncing past his feet. He stabs it with his stick. Thunk thunk – psssst. "The gym block is closed."

More people in hard hats and high-vis vests come into the room. They pop the remaining balls and throw their carcasses into bin bags. Then the hoops are torn down, their nets cut with scissors. Other workers are taking measurements, unscrewing the benches from the sides, peeling the court markings up from the floor.

The whole place has gone from sports site to building site in less than a minute while we all just stand and stare. Once I saw a time-lapse video from when they built the Olympic stadium. This is just like that ... in reverse.

A woman with a clipboard walks right up to Mr Ward. She takes the stopwatch from round his neck and snips its cord. Then she puts it on the floor and with her steel-capped worker boots STAMPS it to smithereens.

"Right, THAT'S IT!" shouts Mr Ward. But the woman just turns and walks away, making a little tick on her clipboard.

"Please stop!" shouts Greg Goldsmith.

"Stop!" "Please!" "Don't!" yells everyone else.

The double doors at the other end of the hall burst open. It's Ms Fortune. She too is wearing a high-vis waistcoat and a yellow hard hat, but hers has got a special extra bit at the back for her bun.

SWEET BUN

"Ah, phew. Ms Fortune," says Mr Ward. "You need to help us. They're wrecking our gym block!"

"No, no..." says Ms Fortune. "There's no need to worry. The gym block isn't being shut down."

"Phew," says everyone, in a collective sigh.

"It's being shut UP!"

"Whu?" says everyone, in a collective confused grunt.

"Yes, UP. UP as in upgrade. Up as in improved. Up as in "The only way is..." Up as in better. This is all part of our renovations programme. We're going to make this place better. Much, much better!"

Now everyone's just confused.

"You like the paint job, and the plants everywhere, don't you?"

"Er..." says everyone.

"Kids don't really care about wall colours that much," says Adele.

"But the goody bags, with the rubbers?"

"Those were great," says Gareth.

WHAT IS HE SAYING???

"Listen, Ms Fortune," says Mr Ward. "It seems to me that what is happening here is not entirely in the best interests of all the students."

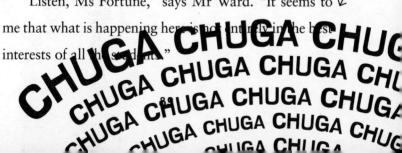

CHUGA CHUGA

CHEW

CRACK
CRUMBLE

Mr Ward is cut short. We turn and there, right in the middle of the hall, are a man and a woman with a pneumatic drill, tearing into the laminated floor. Chunks of wood and dust and cement are flying up all around them.

"IT'S LOUD IN HERE." Ms Fortune smiles. "LET'S GO THROUGH THERE, I CAN TELL YOU WHAT'S IN STORE."

Ms Fortune ushers our whole class out of a side door. Suddenly we are all out in the playground alongside a giant billboard that definitely wasn't here before.

GYM BLOCK 2.0 / SPA EXPERI… 2…AP…

"These are the architects' images," says Ms Fortune, guiding us past the billboard. "Look how happy the little people are! You see, I'm making everything much better. Enriching lives. Any questions?"

"I have a question," says Mr Ward. "Several, in fact."

"None at all?" says Ms Fortune, completely ignoring him. She claps her hands together. "This is fun, isn't it? Now, back to class. This is a restricted access construction site now. You can't be here without hard hats." And with that she goes back into the building. There is the sound of bolts sliding across, locking us out.

We walk back to the main building. The cruel wind of the outside world is whipping across our bare legs as we go, but still: most of us are excited.

"I can't wait to get in the extra-large Jacuzzi!"

"I'm going to get a massage EVERY DAY!"

"I'm going to be more pampered than a baby!"

"Are you guys mad!?" says Sam. "This is all just spa things, like saunas and Jacuzzis. There's nothing on these boards for ACTUAL PE. You know, things like throwing and catching beanbags, hula hooping, playing netball, rounders, football ... stuff like that."

"Who needs it?" says Leo. "We're going to be living the high life when the new spa comes in!"

"Come on, Ms Fortune always promises things but we never actually get them," says Adele.

"You mean like that time she didn't give us those donuts because Tom and Sam smashed the window!? Repairs are expensive!" says Gareth.

"You can see from here that the window has never

been repaired!" says June. "Look! There probably were no donuts in the first place."

A massive CRASH behind us stops the conversation. We look back to see that a wrecking ball has, well, come in like a wrecking ball and smashed into our gym block.

"Goodbye, old gym," says someone.

"Hello, brand new spa!" says another.

They cheer. Everyone is celebrating. Well, almost everyone. I notice that Mr Ward just looks as confused as I feel. Adele and June exchange glances too.

We all watch as the main wall takes one more hit from the wrecking ball, wavers there for a moment like late-stage Jenga and then topples. Bricks crumble. Floorboards crack. Glass shatters. A great cloud of dust blooms upwards. It's smashing. It's crushing.

13 THE BLAME GAME

It's Wednesday morning, a full week on from the gym block demolition. The dust has settled, and so have we. We're in the hall for assembly. Now that Ms Fortune has been here for a little while, assemblies don't have as much razzle-dazzle. There's no dry ice, no spotlights. It's much more basic, like a normal assembly. When Ms Fortune walks out onto the stage she doesn't sing, just says "Good afternoon, children of Belton," like a regular headteacher. Her voice echoes from the speakers.

The applause lights still come on. The hall claps for her, but the enthusiasm has died down a bit since that first time. Some people clap because they still

think Ms Fortune is as wonderful as she says she is. Some clap because they don't want to get in trouble for not clapping.

"Actually, you can all stop that," she says. "I'm not in the mood for celebration today."

Everyone stops immediately.

"Belton, Belton, Belton," she says, shaking her head. "This school. This hallowed place of learning. I've already given you so much. The plants. The paint. The rubbers! And there's so much more to come. The new spa … I mean the gym block, is almost ready. It's looking fantastic, by the way."

I can barely concentrate on what she's saying. I'm still trying to work out what's happening with the voices in my head. All week, I've been clenching my teeth to see what happens. Right now, nothing happens. But then Ms Fortune and Pin and Price and all the teachers are in this room, and it's only ever them I seem to hear in my head. I look around at

the teachers, all sitting in one neat row on a bench at the side. Their neat hairstyles. Their little winkies all on proud display (their winky-face badges, I mean). There's something odd going on here, but I can't work out what.

"But I'm not sure if you guys will be able to use the spa," Ms Fortune continues. "Not sure if I can trust you guys." She sighs. "Not after these latest goings-on. Mr Price?"

Mr Price steps forward. "Will the following children please line up on the centre of the stage."

The screen has four names on it. Everyone gasps as the kids reluctantly go up to the stage.

- Finn
- Deborah
- Susan
- Adele

"Very disappointing." says Ms Fortune. "OK, Mr Price, what do we have here?"

Mr Price reads from a clipboard. "This first child is Finn Adams. He has been chewing gum – with his mouth open, so it makes a horrible noise."

Finn looks around confused. "I ... I ... I only chewed it in the playground, on my own. How did you know?"

"The school is a shared space, boy. We know everything," Ms Fortune says. "You've just lost 100 Fortune Loyalty Points for everyone in the school."

"What!?"

"And all gum is now banned. Thanks to this boy!"

"BOO!" says everyone.

Mr Price keeps reading from his clipboard. "These two girls were reported to be plaiting one another's hair and planning even bolder hairstyles."

Deborah and Susan look at each other, bemused. "I just wanted to try an updo!" says Deborah.

"Nobody was around," says Susan. "We didn't think it would matter."

Ms Fortune cuts across them: "Bold, strange

haircuts can confuse people and could be particularly off-putting to visitors. From now on, because of these two, we have been forced to create a BLAST style guide for hair."

She points at the screen.

BLAST style guide

Permitted hairstyles, in order of preference:

Boys	Girls
Side parting (right)	Bun (tight)
Centre parting	High pony (tight)
Military style buzz cut	Military style buzz cut

Please be sure to AVOID the following

Boys	Girls
"Quiff"	"B___e"
"Bedhead"	"Natural wa___"
"Mullet"	"Fringe"

Now it is Adele's turn.

"And this girl," Mr Price says, consulting his clipboard, "left scraps of food and school rulers all over the classroom floor."

"That was a hamster trap!" says Adele. She is completely ignored.

"OK, no more rulers!" says Ms Fortune. "In fact, all stationery is now banned!"

NO
MASTICATION

NO
"HAIRDOS"

NO
RULERS

NO
BROCCOLI

AGAIN, THIS IS JUST PERSONAL

THIS MEANS CHEWING BTW

There are outbursts of "What?" and "No!" And "What about pencils?"

"The school's image is important, very important," Ms Fortune goes on. "We're going to have outsiders coming in soon. That's part of the unique business model we're setting up. Little piles of rubbish and rulers simply WILL NOT DO. I want you guys to be able to enjoy the wonderful new things which I'm going to bring here, but for that we're going to have to all dig deep, work hard and toe the line together.

"For that reason I've set up a new reporting device to work alongside our existing measures. A special telephone booth has been installed in the hallway. It's called the dob-line. If you suspect anyone of doing anything that may harm the image of the school, you must immediately report it. For the good of everyone! Now, back to class, all of you."

"This is getting ridiculous!" Mr Ward shouts from the back of the hall. "A hotline for tattle-tales?"

One of the new teachers, I think it's Mr Derry, tuts at him and then stands up and gestures for his class to do the same. Soon all the new teachers are standing up and Mr Ward, and his point, are lost behind a forest of people.

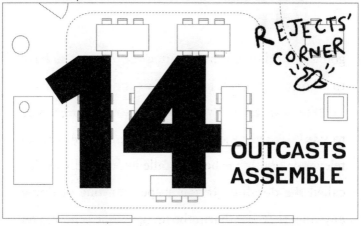

REJECTS' CORNER

14
OUTCASTS ASSEMBLE

Sam and June sit at the back of class with me in what has become "rejects' corner". And now Adele has joined us too, ever since the ruler ban she hasn't been too popular either. She apologized to June straight away and they seem to be friends again. So that's nice.

We are supposed to be making artworks inspired by the Great Fire of London.

The Great Fire of London was a fire in London and it got really good reviews. It was in 1666 and in those days some guy called Samuel Pepys kept a diary, a bit like an olden-days Wimpy Kid. He wrote all about the fire and how he buried his favourite thing – his cheese collection – to keep it safe. So we're making paintings of our favourite things.

SAMUEL PEPYS
1633–1703 • DIARY GUY
(IT'S PRONOUNCED "PEEPS" BTW)

Sam is drawing a chip (potato). Adele is drawing a chip (computer). June is drawing her nana, who played with chips (poker). (Sadly though she is dead so June is drawing a skeleton.) I'd like to draw my new friends, but that would be awkward. Whatever though, none of us are really concentrating. We're too distracted by the assembly we just had.

"That was so weird," says June. "Ms Fortune is mean, making you all get on stage."

"It was horrid, being up there," says Adele.

We all mutter in agreement.

"She's clever though," says Sam. "She's trying to divide us up by singling out 'bad' kids and blaming them for everything. We should let everyone who's been singled out know they're not alone."

"But how?" says June.

"I don't know," says Sam.

I don't say anything, as usual. I'm a bit distracted. While the others are talking I casually try clenching my teeth, and now I can hear Ms Fortune again. *"Keep monitoring those kids,"* she's saying. *"If any of them—"*

"Excuse me." Nucky leans right over me, and I instantly relax my jaw.

"Oh, hi," I say.

"I just wanted to borrow an orange pen," he says.

NUCKY'S MUM
AGE: ?? • REAL NAME: CAROL
SKIN TONE: ORANGE

"Are you drawing your mum?" says Sam. (Nucky's mum is very fond of tanning beds.)

"Actually, I'm making a poster," says Nucky. "I want to get Hammy back. I just need the orange to colour him in."

"That's it!" says Sam. "Posters ... we can do posters!"

"Who's we?" says Nucky.

"Anyone who wants to help the fightback against Ms Fortune's fibs," says Sam.

June shrugs. "I'm in."

"I'm in too," says Adele.

"I just want Hammy back," says Nucky. "It was Pin and Price that lost him. Now he's in danger, probably! In peril, at the very least."

"Good," says Sam. "So you're in too."

Everyone turns to look at me now. Eight expectant eyes. They watch. They wait. Nucky blinks.

"Are you with us, Tom?" says Sam.

"I, er..." I er.

"We've been rejected by everyone since we lost the whole school that load of donuts," says Sam.

"There probably were no donuts!" says Adele. "Ms Fortune is just exploiting her power. Making everyone afraid."

It is pretty bad. Almost ... evil. What else can I say. "In," I say.

The others all smile. June passes round a load of clean sheets of paper. "Let's do this," she says. "We can stick them up on the way to the library later."

"Ooh. Are we a group?" says Nucky, pulling out a chair to join us. "We need a name, don't we?"

"He's right," says Adele. "Like how in *Les Miserables* they're called La Resistance."

"Oh yeah," "Classic," "Love 'Lay Mizz'" say the others, nodding along. How does everyone suddenly know about these things except me?

"So … The Laresistance then?" I say, trying to get back into the conversation.

"Er … maybe," says June, clearly unimpressed. Nucky frowns.

"No, no," I say. I need something better. "What about FAFF? It's like what you said earlier, Sam. Fighting Against Fortune's Fibs."

"Beats The Laresistance." June shrugs. Everyone else nods. FAFF it is! Now it's time to stop faffing about and get down to business. FAFF-business: making Anti-Fortune posters.

Join us! Simply cut out and keep this membership card

F.A.F.F.

Fighting Against Fortune's Fibs

MS FORTUNE #1
MS FORTUNE #1
MS FORTUNE #1
MS FORTUNE #1
MS F   NE #1
MS F   #1
MS   #1
MS FOR UNE #1
MS FORTUNE #1
MS FORTUNE #1

FORTUNE FAVOURS THE OBEDIENT

MS
MS
MS
MS
MS
MS
MS
MS
MS

MY HEAD IS GREAT
MY HEAD IS GREAT
MY HEAD IS GREAT
M
M
M
M
M
M
M
MY HEAD IS GREAT
MY HEAD IS GREAT
MY HEAD IS
MY HEAD IS
MY HEAD IS

PRICE + PIN ARE MEAN!

MS FORTUNE #1
MS FORTUNE #1
MS FORTUNE #1
#1
#1
#1
#1
#1

MY
MY
MY
MY
MY
MY
MY
MY

Ms F is EVIL

A BULLY!

FORTU
FORTU

BRING BAC THAT OTHER GUY!

OUT TO LAUNCH

It's been over a week since we put up our FAFF posters. Well, I say we. I didn't actually do any sticking. Sam and June took the lead on that. But I did help roll out blobs of Blu-Tack in preparation and I used my magic jaw to listen in to Ms Fortune and the others. I wanted to keep June and Sam safe.

I have been listening in a lot more over the last week. So I know that Ms Fortune has no idea who is responsible for the posters. I also know she is really annoyed by them – she's been using some distinctly un-child-friendly words about the whole thing. Like ██████████, ██████████, and even ██████ ██████ ██████████ in the ██████████!

Talk about blue and tacky. But there's absolutely nothing she can do. All that's happened is now there are even more potted plants around, for some reason.

I still haven't told the others about my abilities yet. I haven't found a way of saying it. It's still a secret. It's like a secret superpower, in a way. Maybe superpower is not quite the right word – it's not like I've got laser eyes or anything – but still … it's good. Maybe it's super but in the way a supermarket is super.

There's a bit in Spider-Man where his uncle says "With great power comes great responsibility". This is a small power, so I guess it comes with a small responsibility? I know I should do something. Or tell someone. I just don't know what. Or who. (Or when or where or how.)

SPIDER-MAN

• • •

Everyone's clustered by the entrance to the new gym block because today is the opening day. Everyone is pretty excited about the pool and Jacuzzi. Some of the kids are already wearing their goggles. There's a gang of second years in swimming caps. Leo is wearing *two* verruca socks, one on each foot. How gross do you have to be to have verrucas on both feet?

Everyone is crammed together around the entrance. (Well, there's a little more space by Leo Ness.) Or at least, this used to be the entrance. Now it's been completely bricked over.

Mr Ward comes over to us, his break-time coffee in one hand. "Are you guys sure it's today?" he says, scratching his beard.

"It's definitely today!" says Gareth. "Look – it says OPENING TODAY!"

YAGOT ƎNINƎꟼO

"It says Ya Dot G-nine Po," says June. "Is that … hip-hop speak or something?"

"It says OPENING TODAY! They just put it up backwards," says Ramesh. "You need to relax – shouldn't be too difficult in our new mega Jacuzzi!"

"I can't wait to dive in!"

"I'm going to boil myself like an egg!"

"I'm going to get a hot stone massage!"

"I've got itchy feet," says Leo. The people closest to him edge away. "I mean, I want to go in!" he says, offended. "When can we?"

"I'm sure it won't be too long now," says Mr Ward. "You shouldn't expect too much from the actual opening, though. Often with these things they go for what is known as a 'soft launch', they open it up quietly at first. There's not always a massive fanfare."

BUP-BADA-BUP-BUP -BUP-BAAAAAAA

Suddenly, from the other side of the building, there comes a massive fanfare.

"What the heck!?" says Sam. "They're on the wrong side!"

Over the wall, we can just about make out the top bits of a full marching band. Massive feathers on their hats, that bit of a trombone that goes back and forth going back and forth, a tossed baton loop-de-looping in the air above them.

"There's loads of people over there!" shouts Nucky. He has used his parkour skills to climb the mesh fencing in front of the wall. "Hey! Guys, excuse me! Oi!"

"Eek!" says someone on the other side of the wall.

"Oh no – a child!" says another.

"Yeah, hi!" says Nucky. "You guys are on the wrong side!"

"Young man, please stop haranguing us," says another voice from the crowd beyond the wall.

"What?" says Nucky.

And then...

BANG!

I gasp! What was that?

"OMG they shot Nucky!" says Glen. "Nooooooo!" he cries, falling to his knees.

Then there's another SNAP! and suddenly the sky is full of shimmering silver sparkles.

"It's fireworks!" says Nucky. Glen gets to his feet looking a bit embarrassed.

CRACKLE! POP! More fireworks! Actual fireworks, in the middle of the day. And they're on the wrong side of the building too!

"Aaaaah!" say all the kids at once.

BOOM! A confetti cannon shoots coloured paper into the air.

"Ooooh!" say the kids this time. Not me though. I want to find out what's happening so I clench my jaw. Now I can hear Ms Fortune – she's in my head again.

"I need to get rid of those kids. They're disturbing the grand opening."

Then I hear her again, but with my ears this time. She's behind us. She's riding one of those hoverboard things. She cruises right through the middle of us, bumping kids out of the way. "Will you brats stop making such a racket!" she shouts, spinning on the spot... The sunlight catches on her shimmering diamond earrings and thick gold necklace, she's like Henry VIII with more bling. Where did all that come from?

HENRY VIII
1491–1547 • KING OF ENGLAND
LIKES: WEDDINGS, FUNERALS

"We're here for the new gym," says Rohan.

"For opening day ... it's today," says June.

"Ahahaha, the gym is open!" says Ms Fortune. "But Phase One is members only."

112

"Are WE members?" says Greg. And then, more excitedly, "I have a card! Is this a membership card?" He holds his loyalty card as high as he can, a tiny flag.

"Ha, no, no. Those cards don't mean anything. Membership is for pre-approved high net-worth individuals aged 21 or over ... which sadly rules all of you out on every single count." Ms Fortune smiles.

"Oh." Greg's flag drops down. Everyone is disappointed.

"What about Mr Ward?" says Tina. "He's really old!"

"He still buys music. In shops!" adds Glen, for emphasis.

"Not exactly a high-roller, though, are you, Mr Ward?" says Ms Fortune. "I know what you get paid, don't forget."

"I…" says Mr Ward. And then, quietly, "No." He's gone red. Like what I do.

"That's just how we have to start things off. These things are expensive, so we need to recoup some of the money before we can open up the building to everyone. Remember we talked before about A/B use? It's standard practice. For now it's just group A – the professionals. Obviously, that's not you."

"You guys are B. B minors, actually. That means that for now you really should 'B' away from here. Back inside the main school building."

"What, why?" says Mr Ward.

"The clients don't want to look at children when they arrive."

"Will loyalty points get us in sooner?" asks Tina. "I've got loads!"

Ms Fortune frowns and then tilts her head into her

collar. That's weird. She looks like she's talking into the winky badge on her jacket. What is she...? Then I see it. A tiny wire – as thin as a hair – running from the badge up to her ear.

The cheeky winky is a walkie-talkie! Suddenly everything falls into place. I'm not psychic or telepathic. The teachers are using some kind of radio built into their badges to communicate with each other. They're using them to spy on us! And for some reason, I can tune into them!

16

FLAG UP

The teachers have secret walkie-talkies so they can talk to one another. And somehow I can hear what they're saying too! Wow. This is crazy. This is mega. I have to tell someone. But then: this is me... I don't tell people things! Especially big, crazy mega news-items like this. I need to be sure. Who would believe me anyway? They'd think I was talking a load of—

"Pants," says a voice from behind me.

"Whu?" I say, turning on the spot. It's Nucky! He has a bundle of sheets under his arm. Sam is with him too. I thought I was alone in the playground. Everyone else is back inside. They all trudged off, moaning about the gym.

"Er ... pants?" I say. That is an advanced-level conversation starter. "You mean the gym block thing? Yeah, it's pretty bad."

"It's really bad," says Sam. "That's why we're going to do something about it."

"Pants!" says Nucky again.

"We've got an idea. Nucky saw Ms Fortune and Mr Price and Mr Pin go into the spa," says Sam. "He snuck in to the changing rooms and stole these!"

"They're Mr Price's," says Nucky proudly, unfurling his bundle to reveal a great pair of pants. Actual PANTS.

Y-FRONTS

"It's time for FAFF to take action again!"

Y AS IN WHY IS NUCKY SHOWING ME A MASSIVE PAIR OF MANKY PANTS?

"Come on!" says June.

"Er…" I say. "Me?" I feel uncomfortable already.

"It's a FAFF mission!" says Sam.

"I … I guess I could be on lookout?" I say. "What's the plan?"

"YES! You're in!" says Nucky. "You'll love it! Come on, we'll explain it on the way."

The five of us hurry round the school building. They tell me the plan as we go. I can't believe they're

going to do it. I can't believe I know people who do things like this. Ms Fortune is going to flip her lid when she sees it. I really, really, really hope they don't get caught.

I clench my jaw, but this time I can't hear any talking. There's just a weird distant bubbling sound. That must be the Jacuzzi, that's it. And even that is so faint I might be making it up. So the coast is clear for now.

We get to the flagpole. It looks impossibly tall. From here at the bottom the flag is little more than one of those squiggly hyphens (~).

"Oh, well. It was a bit of a weird idea anyway," I say.

"Don't go, Tom! We're still going to do it," says Adele. "We just need to work together!"

"June, can you untie that rope?" Sam points to the rope hanging down from the flag. It's tied to the pole, all the way up.

"A frayed knot," says June, inspecting it. "And yes, of course I can."

She puts her index finger on the knot, twists one of the ends, pushes another bit through and – voila – the knot falls apart.

"Nice one!" says Nucky.

"I might need some help for the next one though," June says. We all look up to the next tie point, a couple of metres up.

Nucky puts his hands against the flagpole. "Climb on!"

June clambers up onto Nucky's shoulders and begins untying the higher knot.

"OK, next one," says June. "Climb up, Adele, I'll tell you how to do it."

Without a pause Adele clambers up past Nucky and onto June's shoulders.

The three of them neatly stack together like a human version of George the window cleaner's ladder.

"OK," says June. "Just put a finger on the big loop ... hold the top rope, and twist!"

119

"It worked!" says Adele. The next bit of rope tumbles free.

I look around, I listen in. The coast is still clear.

"There's just one more to go," says Sam. "My turn!" He actually wants to do this! He makes his way to the top of the tower, all ready to untie the final knot. But when he reaches up for it he's just shy. (Welcome to my world!) He can't reach it! "If everyone just moves a bit closer to the pole, I'll get it," he calls down. Nucky takes a shaky step forwards, everyone sways. I bite down again and this time I can hear lots of action. The rustling of fabric on microphones. Muffled, serious conversations. Snatches of instructions. I hear Ms Fortune saying *"Serge, sweep the playground … start at the east side."* The east side is where we are now! The others are going to get caught. We need to get out of here.

"We've got to go!" I say, urgently. "Now."

"Just a minute." Sam is still straining to reach the last knot.

"No, we've got to go NOW!" I say.

"Have you seen someone?" says Nucky, looking about and making the human tower wobble even more.

This is useless. If I help them, maybe we'll all get away quicker. Without giving myself any time to go over the idea, I start climbing.

I hook my knee onto Nucky's outstretched arm. I use Sam's hood as a foot hold. I pull on Adele's leg and from there, somehow, I head for Sam's shoulders. I am like a clumsy uncool Spider-Man, working my way up to the top of the stack.

"Yes!" says June as I reach for the final knot. "It's exactly the same – finger on the big loop – hold the top rope, and TWIST!" I follow the instructions and the knot falls apart effortlessly.

The rope holding the flag up tumbles free like Rapunzel's hair.

"Hooray!" says our human tower.

"Now let's go!" I say. "PLEASE!" I begin to climb down, accidentally kicking Sam in the face.

"What the!" he says, jerking his head back.

"Uh oh..." calls Adele. Everything gets wibblier and wobblier. We crash down.

WHAM! WHOMF! CRASH! BAM!

We are a tangled heap of kids. My left arm is caught in a knot of limbs. My face is pressed against an armpit. I think I'm sitting on someone's head.

"Well, we got the rope free!" says Sam from within the heap.

I clench my teeth again and hear Mr Pin. *"There's some activity round by the flagpole,"* he says.

"Oh no!" I shout. "They're coming!"

"It's fine!" says Nucky. "Let's do the flag."

"We have to go NOW!" I say.

Quickly June knots the pants to the rope, and then pulls. With each tug of the rope, the pants are pulled higher. Soon the pants are flying up, up, up!

The official flag drops into a puddle on the dirty floor. In its place at the top of the pole is a new flag, a great fluttering pair of PANTS. They dance on the breeze, the bright sun glowing through them. Brown speckles dance in the light. A stain spangled banner. But there's no time to admire it.

"Trust me," I say. "Please! We have to go now!" I drag them all to the main building, glancing briefly over my shoulder to catch sight of the new flag again. And there is Mr Pin. He is looking at the pants. He doesn't look happy.

I clench my jaw. *"What the... Ms Fortune, you're not going to believe what someone's done to the flag!"*

17 RE-RE-STRUCTURE

We walk through the main building into the playground for the rest of lunch break. The others are all chatting around me.

"I can't believe we got away with it!" says Sam.

"That was so close," June adds.

"Yeah," says Adele. "Lucky for us we had Tom. It was like you just knew Mr Pin was going to appear, Tom. Amazing."

"I did know," I say quietly. "I... Er... Listen. It's..." Come on, Tom. Now or never. "They have secret teacher walkie-talkies and somehow I can hear what they're saying," I say in a rush.

There's a silence and then:

"What?"

"You can hear them? How?"

"Walkie-talkies?"

"Is she mad?"

"Hang on," says Sam. "Let her speak. Explain, Tom. What do you mean? They're using hidden walkie-talkies? And you can hear them??"

"Well, yeah ... pretty much," I say. "When I clench my teeth, I can hear what the teachers say. It's like magic, or something. A superpower. But ... not that super. It's nothing, probably. I don't know why. It's been going on for a couple of weeks."

"You haven't told ANYONE?! For WEEKS? Why wouldn't you say something sooner?" says June.

"I wanted to! It's ... well. It's a lot."

"It happens when you clench your teeth?" Adele says. "Can I see?" I don't say anything, but I open up. She is staring at the space between my nose and chin that I normally do anything I can to keep people away from. It's strangely personal, but not completely in a bad way. "It must be the braces," Adele says after a minute.

"The wha...?" I say, my mouth still open.

"They're steel, right?"

"Uh … yeah."

"Well … any closed conductive loop can be a diode and would work as a radio receiver," says Adele, who knows science words like conductive loop and diode and receiver.

"What does that mean?" I say.

"An aerial," says Adele.

"Little mermaid?" says Nucky. We're really bad at this.

"An antenna. Like for the radio. It means you're not reading minds, Tom, you're picking up the radio waves," says Adele. "Here, pass me your exercise book and I'll show you."

I hand over my book and Adele flips to the back pages. I'm just glad the attention is off me for a moment, and I can shut my mouth again.

Adele draws a diagram.

"Tom, clenching your teeth together completes the loop. The braces come together and become a receiver, picking up whatever radio signals are around. Here that means the teachers' walkie-talkie communications!"

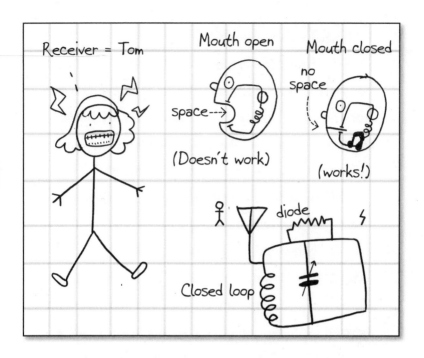

"Woah," says Nucky. "This is big."

"This is GREAT!" says Adele.

"It is!" agrees Sam. "The teachers use those walkie-talkies to talk about us – but now we can listen to them!"

Everyone's eyes are fixed on me. I've never been looked at by anyone for this long. I feel like a TV screen. It's .... kind of awkward. "What are they talking about now?" says Sam.

Slowly I clench my teeth.

"I can hear Ms Fortune and Mr Price," I report. "Mr Price is getting his pants back. Ms Fortune isn't happy about it. They don't know who to blame. They're saying it must have been someone very tall. They're saying... Oh no!" I clench my teeth harder. "They think Mr Ward had something to do with the pants! They're going to fire him!"

I can't believe it.

Sam, June, Adele and Nucky are alongside me, reading the newsletter pinned to our classroom door. We're all in shock. Mr Ward ... gone?

"Beach balls," mutters Adele, eventually.

"That evil..." says June.

"Is this because of the flag?" whispers Nucky.

"It must be..." says Sam, keeping his voice low. He seems really upset. "It's all our fault—"

"First we lost Hammy, now we've lost Mr Ward too..." says Nucky.

ISSUE #2　　　　　　　　　　　　"FREE"

The Belton Bugle

THE BELTON LUXCORP® ACADEMY OF STUDENT TEACHING™ NEWSLETTER

★ ★ ★ ★ SPECIAL EDITION ★ ★ ★ ★
Farewell to Mr Ward
BEARDY TEACHER TO LEAVE SCHOOL
WITH IMMEDIATE EFFECT

Mr Ward has decided to leave the Belton Luxcorp© Academy of Student Teaching™ after he was asked to leave. His last day was today.

We say thank you to Mr Ward for all his work in service of the school. "Mr Ward has been at Belton Luxcorp Academy of Student Teaching for a long time,"

Mr Ward was always quite ... low-res

said Ms Fortune in a statement. "He's been a very persistent teacher."

"And can I flag up that his most recent has been a banner year, in which he's gone way beyond the standard," she continued.

Coming Soon! ## The Library®
A Curated Fruit Drink Experience
YES, THERE WILL BE BOOKS!

18 BORROWED TIME

It's Tuesday. Class library time. Mr Ward called it BRILL – as in Belton Readers In Lending Library. I can't imagine it's going to be that BRILL with our new teacher – Ms Perry. No one's seen her this morning, though, so we're heading to the library on our own.

Still, there's some excitement. There's a new book out in our favourite series, "Headless Chickens." They're poultry-based horrors by Paige Turner (not her real name). They're such good books. Almost as good as TV!

Then Greg Goldsmith says something about the library door being stuck. He can't open it.

"I'll do it," says Nucky, pushing his sleeves up as he makes his way to the front of the small crowd.

"Oh ... hold on," he says, wrestling with the handle. "Just a sec..." he's getting worked up now. He puts his foot up on the wall. He's yanking like crazy, but the door is completely unmoving. It might as well be a mural.

"You can do it, Nucky!" shouts Greg, encouragingly.

"We believe in you!" shouts someone else. Now people are cheering. "Come on!"

"Open her up!"

"Floor that door!
Floor that door!
Floor that door!"

we chant.

There is more cheering and arm waving. Wolf whistles! An attempt at a Mexican wave! Actual ticker tape showers down on us, like in a New York parade.

Wait ... what?

I look up. There really are bits of paper drifting down over our small crowd. But they're not the candy colours of confetti – just the papery colour of paper.

There's some writing on it.

"Why did you do it, Clive?" sobbed Melanie.
"There's only one reason," said Clive, glancing his chicken eyes upwards. "Because I love you."
"Oh, Clive. But ... the zombies!"

I know this! It's from *DeadBeak Dad* – "Headless Chickens" #12. What the walnut?

More and more paper fragments fall down. A piece drifts down and sticks to Nucky's forehead. "What the... ?" he says as a second piece sticks on to his cheek. His sweat is making them glue in place. He peels the scraps from his face and starts walking round the building to where all the bits are coming from. Everyone follows close behind.

"WHAT THE...?" he says again – but in capital letters this time – as he turns the corner. There are gasps from the rest of us too as we catch up with him.

The scene before us is like something out of a horror movie ... for books.

SKREEEECH!

19

SCREECH POWERS

We dash round to the other side of the library and find ... a building site. NO ENTRY tape and trucks and cement mixers and workers standing round, you know: building site stuff.

The paper is being spewed from a piece of machinery right in the middle of everything. A cross between a photocopier and a monster truck. Across its side, in giant red letters, is written SHREDMASTER 3000.

A worker in a high-vis jacket comes out of the library's side door and hurls a stack of books into the machine. It screeches in gratitude.

It heaves and shudders,
steam jets from its chimney,
and then a puff of shredded
paper is spat out into the air.

"Our books!"

"Our brill books!"

"STOP!"

"STOP!"

"STOP!"

RIP!   *TEAR!*

SKREEEEEEEEEEEE

SHRED!

SHRED MASTER 3000

"Ahahaha-ha," comes a voice. Ms Fortune smiles widely as she drops down in front of us. She is riding a cherry picker platform attached to a mechanical arm.

"You guys don't need to worry," she says. "This is all for you! We are making space for a NEW library!"

"But those are our books!" says Greta.

"The new library will have more than just books!" says Ms Fortune. "There will be Wi-Fi and lamps and sofa-seating and we will serve SO MANY fresh health-smoothies!"

"But ... our stories," says Greta.

"There *will* be storeys," says Ms Fortune, patting Greta on the top of the head. "Two storeys – the ground floor for customers, and then a mezzanine level to access the extra-extra-large blender we're getting. For the smoothies."

"But ... but we love the library as it is!" shouts Lee.

"As it *was*, little boy. As it was. This is progress! A better library for everyone," says Ms Fortune. "All in line with our corporate policy."

This is too much. How can we be expected to believe in all this after so many let downs?

"Corporate policy?" says Sam. "This is a SCHOOL!"

"It's an Academy of Student Teaching, thank you."

"You haven't finished the gym yet!" says June.

"The gym is finished. It's going terrifically well already," says Ms Fortune. "One client said it's 'the best prem-lux spa this side of Bath' and gave it five out of five bubbles on Treats4Elites.com."

A client? Prem-lux?? What are these things!?

"But the door is still bricked over," says Nucky. "Nobody from the school has even been in it!" He's getting red in the face all over again.

"Nobody from the *Academy of Student Teaching*. And one of you has, at least," she says, glaring at us. "We doubt Mr Wart was

working alone." Oh, yeah … the stolen pants.

"Now look, this is a private construction site. It's very dangerous, you really shouldn't be round here. It's 'totes inappropes'. You'll have to go and read your little books in my classroom."

"In our classroom, you mean?" says Nucky, exasperated.

"Just go," says Ms Fortune. "Where is your teacher? Ah, Ms Perry, there you are. Please take these children away." And what can we do? We trudge back to class, paper still fluttering down on top of us.

The furious chicken slides in for the tackle.

CRACK!

SEEN SOMETHING?

SAY SOMETHING!

TALKING IN THE HALLWAYS? NO WAY!

We must be considerate of the Private Clients who share our space.

WANTED

An indecent act was carried out involving the flagpole and the intimate clothing of an esteemed member of staff.

Did you see anything?Use the dob-line to report them as soon as possible.

The Library®
A Curated Fruit Drink Experience

After your spa experience at Belton Bubbles, join us at THE LIBRARY® for a healthy & delicious premium luxe fruit drink experience.

OPENING SOON!

20 NEST IN PEACE

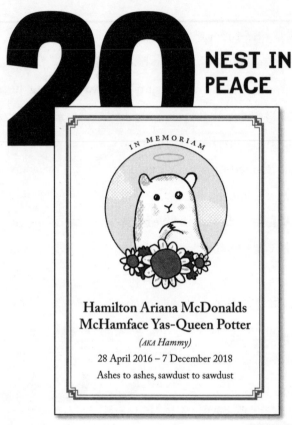

IN MEMORIAM

Hamilton Ariana McDonalds McHamface Yas-Queen Potter

(AKA Hammy)

28 April 2016 – 7 December 2018

Ashes to ashes, sawdust to sawdust

What a week it's been. We've heard nothing from Mr Ward and Ms Perry is a terrible teacher. She never remembers anyone's name, and she thinks a well-earned treat is opening the window. Teachers are supposed to inspire – she couldn't inspire a turd to stink! So it's all rather gloomy anyway, but it's doubly so because we're at a funeral.

It's quite hard to make out exactly what he's saying toward the end, what with all the sobbing.

"That was nice, Nuck," says June.

Nucky clears his throat and wipes the mucus from his face with his sleeve. We just stand there, staring at the tiny wooden gravestick. Nucky pulls a battered orange beanbag with a face drawn on from his pocket. "Goodnight, old bean," he whispers to it. "I'll never forget you." He's been carrying this around for weeks. He says it reminds him of Hammy.

"You'll be alright, Nucky." June pats him on the shoulder and smiles at him. It's a lovely, tender moment, though maybe it would be easier to watch if Nucky didn't have a giant snot bubble coming out of his left nostril.

"Here, everyone take some of these," says Sam, holding out a sandwich bag of pumpkin seeds. One by one we scatter them over the "grave".

"Goodbye, furry friend."

"Nest in peace."

"Farewell, tiny hamster."

"You were wizard, Hammy."

More sobbing

In a way, it's just 30–50 old
seeds and a lolly stick.

But in another way, it's
the most heartbreakingly
beautiful thing ever.

21

END OF THE DAY

It's the end of the school day. Not a moment too soon. What a day. We've been sad about Hammy all afternoon. I'm ready to go home.

I find Mum in the playground. "Hey," I say.

"Hey," huffs Mum. "Just a second, yeah?" She taps the phone screen a couple more times, and then finally turns to me. "Everything all right, angel?"

"Er, not really, Mum. I've got a new head. It's—"

"Oh, I'm sure you can brush that out," she says, glancing up at my hair.

"My headteacher, Mum! Ms Fortune. She fired Mr Ward. And she closed the library. And I think she's got a secret plan that she's not telling—"

"Ms Fortune! Oh, I know all about her," says Mum. "She's all over my newsfeed – look!"

Mum holds out her phone.

New School Gym is
AMAZING!!!

5 more notifications

MumsWeb.com • 4 mins ago
35 Surprising Reasons Why
Everyone LOVES Ms Fortune

13 more notifications

Belton Buzz • 6 mins ago
A Woman Took Over a
School. You Won't BELIEVE
What Happened Next!

99+ more notifications

"The new gym sounds amazing," says Mum, just as June walks past with her dad.

"I wouldn't know. We're not allowed in it!" I say.

"Oh. I only read the headlines," says Mum.

June's dad stops. "You kids aren't allowed in your own gym?"

"YES, Dad," June says, "That's what I've been trying to tell you for ages! Ms Fortune is horrible and won't let us do anything."

"Everyone LOVES Ms Fortune," says another passing parent.

"Ms Fortune?" chips in another. "I still use the tote bag she gave us when she started as head. Look!"

"Mr Hooper never gave us as much as a carrier bag," says another. "And look at all these plants she's put about the place. Gorgeous."

There's a big group of kids and parents all around us now.

"They said they'd open the gym for adults and kids but it's been ages and it's STILL just for adults!" June says to her dad.

Tina is walking past with her dad now. "You kids still can't go in there?" says Tina's dad. "Sugarplum, why didn't you say anything?"

Tina glares at me and June. "It's fine, Dad. Don't worry about it. The school is using a new model or something. We have a new bench and I can go on it because I have over 1000 points."

"This doesn't seem right," says Tina's dad. "I'm going to go and check."

"Don't, Dad," says Tina. "I'll lose my points!" but it's too late. Other parents are involved now, and there's nothing quite as unstoppable as a bunch of Concerned Parents. Pretty soon every adult is involved. There are worried mutterings that bubble over into troubled chatter and all the way into full-volume shouts. "Won't someone please think of the children!" and "Outrageous!" and "My special flower NEEDS the best so she can bloom!"

"Let's just go and find out what's happening!" says June's dad. He turns back towards the school building and the whole pack of parents follows him. They're almost at the main door when a voice calls.

"Yoo-hoo!" It's Ms Fortune in a sing-song voice she never uses with us. She's smiling so hard her eyes are forced up into two dark crescents. "Are you fine people looking for me? How wonderful – please come over to The Library. I want to show you all something!"

22 SMOOTH OPERATORS

Ms Fortune shows the parents into the new building. It's the library, but not as we know it. The building is the same shape but inside it's all exposed brickwork and statement lighting. There are zero books. Nary a pamphlet. The place that used to be non-fiction is now a counter. Biographies is now baked goods. Fiction is tables and chairs. Celebrity kids books are the toilets.

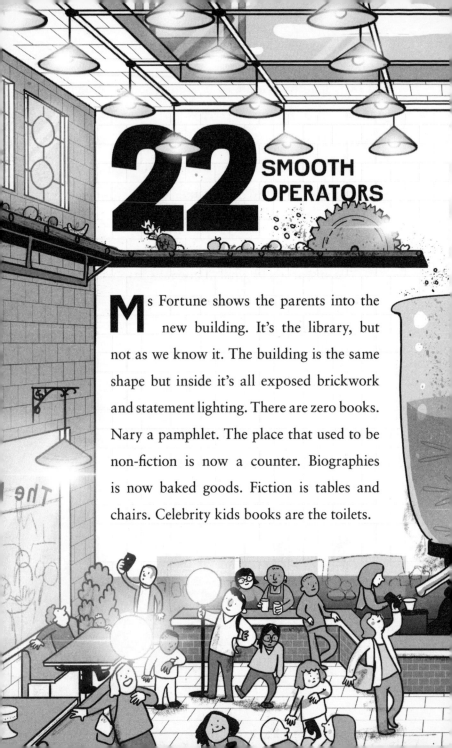

"Wow!" say the parents. "Incredible."

"I love it here," says another, wistfully stroking the back of a chair.

"Look at the lights! This is what I want in the living room!" she says, taking a photo of the ceiling.

"It even has a retractable roof!" says a dad. "Just like Wimbledon!" He presses a button on one wall and the roof slides open to reveal the old school bell and the bright blue sky beyond. Sunlight floods the space, everything glitters with newness.

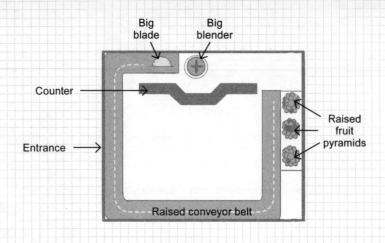

Big blade · Big blender

Counter

Raised fruit pyramids

Entrance →

Raised conveyor belt

"And look at all that fruit ... and the smoothie machine!" someone says.

High above everyone's heads, there is a row of giant pyramids made of different fruits. It's like Ancient Egypt sponsored by Del Monte.

Running below the fruit pyramids is a conveyor belt that carries the fruit towards a massive MASSIVE, MASSIVE blender that sits at floor level. It's an absolute unit – a great glass jug the size of a tank. And not a fish tank, which would be more reasonable – an army tank. The mean kind.

A giant spinning buzzsaw slices through the fruit before it drops into the main blender, where it is blitzed to smithereens by more spinning blades.

The Library®
SLOPS
This is a waste product Do not eat

152

The pulp that comes out slooshes down two chutes – the waste product is funnelled off to a bin marked SLOPS, the rest goes to the counter.

"Anyone for a SMOOTHIE?" Ms Fortune says.

"OOOOOOooooOh," says pretty much everyone, except Tina's dad, who puts his hand up. "What's happened to all the books?" he asks.

"Free smoothies for everyone!" says Ms Fortune, talking over him. "Just order at the counter."

The parents fight and jostle to get to the counter, excitedly scanning the menu board.

"Wait!" says Tina's dad. "Shouldn't a school library have books?"

"Oh, we have books!" says Ms Fortune, pulling out a sheaf of flyers. "Here, have a voucher!"

The Library®

A Curated Fruit Drink Experience

YES!

WE HAVE BOOKS!

Banana • Oatmeal • Olive • Kale • Smoothie

VIP introductory price!
132% of regular price

NB The Library FDE is operated in partnership with Luxcorp Inc.
ALSO PLEASE NOTE we don't have any actual
books, The Library® is just a name.

Tina's dad looks bemused, but any further protests are drowned out by the oohs and aahs of the parents as they drink their smoothies.

"Oh wow, amazing!"

"Totally delish!"

"That is tasty as heck!"

"Wow," says Tina's dad, taking a big gulp of smoothie. "What's in this thing?"

"Dad," Tina says, "what about our books?"

Her dad squints at her as if he can't quite remember who she is. His eyes are round, one pupil slightly bigger than the other. "It's OK, Tina. Daddy is talking to the grown-ups. You know, darling, you're my best—" * burp *

All the parents are completely distracted by their smoothies.

"This is crazy!" shouts one kid, before being hushed by their mum.

"It's totally stupid!"

"It's not a library at all."

"It's a lie, bro!"

"Our library has been turned into a stupid stinking cafe!" says another, before their dad puts his non-smoothie-holding hand over her mouth.

"Ahaha, it's fine, really," says Ms Fortune, her hands up, her eyes half-closed. "But I should say that the scent, Pebbledash Breeze, tested very well in our consumer research. And it's not a cafe, it's The Library – a curated fruit drink experience!"

"I hope to see you all again very soon. Good bye." She holds open the door and the parents follow her lead, back out into the playground.

• • •

We're walking down the hill again, the same throng of parents and kids. But this time all the adults are slurping up a smoothie from a plastic cup, branded as THE LIBRARY. None of them have any more to say about books or gyms. Every single parent has been placated by fruit slurry through a straw.

Mum took a smoothie as well but she's too distracted by her phone to drink any of it.

"Mum..." I whisper urgently. "There's something wrong at the school."

"Sorry, what?" says Mum. She lifts a single earbud out.

"Changes are happening, Mum. Big ones. I'm worried."

Mum stops still. She turns off her phone and this time she actually puts it in her handbag. "Oh, darling, I get it." She smiles as she kneels down in front of me.

"Don't worry. I know. You're at a *magical age*."

"Er..." I say.

A magical what now?

"I've got you covered. I know what this is all about."

Does she? What's she got?

Mum rummages in her handbag. "I've kept this for you all this time. It's very old. It's very special." She looks down for a moment, swallows meaningfully. "I've been waiting for this moment. I think you're ready." She pulls a mysterious package from her handbag. It's delicately wrapped in a piece of old fabric. What did she say – old, special, magical? It must be a mysterious, wonderful heirloom. An enchanted pock-et-watch that stops time? A music-box that grants wishes? Something like that.

I take it in both hands. It's heavy. Wow.

MYSTERIOUS!
EXCITING!
STRANGE!

I slowly turn it over in my hand. The fabric wrapping has a message embroidered onto it. I run my fingers across the letters. S ... P ... O. Oh wait, SPORTS. It says SPORTS. It's a sock. One of Mum's old grey sports socks. I shake it open. Something heavy and black falls into my hand. It's Mum's old phone, from before her latest upgrade. It's been sitting in the kitchen drawer for about three years.

"You enjoy it," says Mum, smiling as if she's just given me the most wonderful gift. She musses up my hair as she stands up, replacing her earbud as she does.

"Thanks," I mutter, and take the phone from her. I click it on. There's no sim card in it so it doesn't even have the internet or work as a phone. It's as dumb as a smartphone gets – just the basics, like a calculator, voice memos and Mum's stupid old game collection. iGiveup.

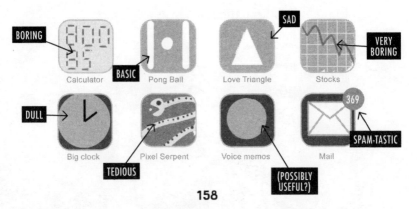

Mum keeps going down the road. I stand there. I look down at my hands, a rank smoothie and an old phone. I don't want either. I stuff the phone into my trouser pocket and pour the drink into a plant pot hanging on the school railings.

Pops and snaps come from the soil. Then a *frzzzzztttt* and a tiny puff of smoke.

The buzzing stops, the leaves droop. I'm no plant expert but that's definitely … odd. I push back a leaf. A glowing red eye stares back at me. Is it … a rat? A robotic rat, sent from the future to kill – oh no, wait … it's the flashing light of a microphone!

23

BUGS LIFE

I'm dying to tell the others what I know as soon
as ASAP. I don't do social media (don't @ me), so
it has to be in person. The moment I get to class the
next day, Sam, Nucky, June and Adele are in rejects'
corner.

I pull a notecard from
my pocket and put it on
the table.

→ DON'T SAY
ANYTHING.

"What?" says Sam.

I place another
notecard on top of it.

→ I'M SERIOUS!
DON'T SPEAK!

I jab at the card with
my finger, waggling my
eyebrows.

I put out another card. →

THE PLANTS
HAVE BUGS.

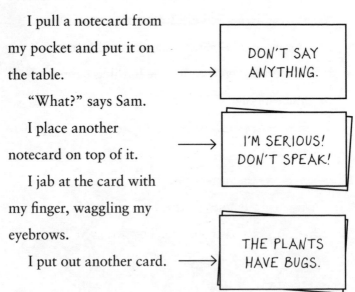

"What are you on about?" says Sam.

I widen my eyes, a finger up to my lips. Nucky, June and Adele are here now too. I point out the cards to them. They all frown, but they're paying attention.

"All plants have bugs," says Nucky.

I put out another card.   And another:

"Woah," says Sam, under his breath.

Another card:

I look over to the front of the class. Ms Perry turns a page in her book. Satisfied that she's distracted, I push back the leaves of the nearest potted plant. There, nestled among the foliage, just as with the other one, is a microphone. The little red light above it pulses like an evil zit.

The others gasp. Each of them scribbles onto bits of paper and holds them up.

Exactly! I try to say, with my eyes.

"This is unbelievable," whispers Adele.

"How did you find out?" says June.

Before I can answer, a terrifying horror-movie style scream rocks the windows.

SHRIEEEEEEeeeEEEEeeeEEEEKKK!!!

"What was that?" The whole class rushes to the window. We see dozens of grown-ups running out of the library building. Some have laptops under their arms, some have cups in their hands, all have panic in their eyes. What is happening?

"Can we go and see?" Sam asks Ms Perry.

"No!" snaps Ms Perry, still in her seat. "Get on with your little doodles."

"Tom, tell us what's happening," Sam whispers.

I clench my teeth. I can hear sobbing. *"It was SO DISGUSTING!"* says a woman's voice. *"DIRTY. HORRIBLE."*

Ms Fortune is with her, doing her best soothing voice. *"Please, Ms Larson. Please calm down. You must be mistaken. We take cleanliness and hygiene very seriously at The Library Curated Fruit Drink Experience."*

I scribble onto the back of a note card, and show it to the others. ———————→

> A woman is v v v upset. Ms F trying to calm her down. Something dirty.

"Why?" says June.

Ms Larson is still talking. *"It had horrible, evil black eyes. And great big pink ears. And a disgusting twitchy pink nose. Gross black markings in an exclamation mark! IT WAS A RAT I KNOW WHAT I SAW IT WAS A RATTY RAT RAT!!!!"*

"Please, Ms Larson. Do not worry. Come down from there, and let me get you a nice drink of water."

"From that kitchen??!?" shouts Ms Larson. *"You might as well offer me a steaming bowl of faeces! Eurgh!"*

"It's a rat," I repeat to the others in a whisper. "Black eyes, pink ears, exclamation-mark black markings..."

"Hammy!" shouts Nucky suddenly. "That's Hammy! He's no rat. He's our friend ... and he's alive!" He stands up. "HAMMY'S ALIVE!"

"Sit down, Nucky!" shouts Ms Perry. "What ARE you getting so excited about? And who is this Harry?"

The rest of the class look at each other, confused. "What's going on?" a couple of them murmur.

"Hammy?"   "Our Hammy?"   "He's alive!?"

"Class, quiet, please," Ms Perry says.

"It's Hammy!" shouts Nucky. "Tom heard it all. He's in the library! The customers think it's a rat in the library, but it's not. It's Hammy!"

Oh crumbs.

"Hammy!" a few kids shout. Soon it becomes a cheer, and as one we dash out of the classroom, ignoring Ms Perry's shouts to stop.

• • •

We push through the open doors of the library, Ms Perry dashing to catch up with us. The space is empty of customers, except for one very distressed woman standing on a table. This must be Ms Larson. She is waving her phone like a flare. "JUST WAIT TILL I POST THIS ONLINE! My followers are going to be VERY interested."

"NO!" shouts Ms Fortune. "NO! Please! Not that. I can make this right. Please." Her cheeks are red. It's the most flustered I've ever seen her. "Just give me the phone."

Ms Larson leaps backwards, shrieking, "Don't touch me! I'll sue.

Don't touch me!

Don't touch me!"

Just then Mr Pin emerges from the kitchen with a Tupperware box. "I got it!" he says, holding the box high. "It *is* a rat!"

"I knew it!!!" shouts Ms Larson. "You wait till my followers hear about this." Then she jumps down from the table and runs out of the building before anyone can stop her.

"YOU, IDIOT!" Ms Fortune shouts to Mr Pin. "Just take that thing to my office so I can DEAL WITH IT. Make sure it doesn't escape! We can't let it ruin things for us."

"On it!" says Mr Pin as he makes his way out of the room.

"Hey!" shout the kids.

"That's Hammy!" shouts Nucky. But Mr Pin ignores them. He's wrapping a roll of grey duct tape round and round the box as he goes. A tight, dark box is no place for our hamster. Mr Price goes with him.

TINY AIRHOLES

NO NATURAL LIGHT

SMELLS OF OLD SOUP

Ms Fortune turns to us kids. "YOU!" she says, "WHAT ARE YOU DOING HERE??"

"That's no rat. It's a hamster. Our hamster!" says Nucky.

"I'm so sorry for the interruption, Ms Fortune," says Ms Perry, finally arriving in the room and glaring at Nucky. "They just ran out of class when they heard about the hamster."

Ms Fortune's brow furrows. "What do you mean 'when they heard about the hamster'?"

"I … er…" Ms Perry pauses. "One of them said something about Tom having heard it. I don't know…"

"Tom heard it…" Ms Fortune says, thoughtfully, and for a second she stares right at me.

Then there's a cry of delight near by. Sean has picked up an old smoothie glass and is drinking from it. "Wow, this really is delicious."

Ms Fortune rounds on him. "Stop what you are doing AT ONCE. That is not for you!" she yells.

"Ugh, kids are disgusting! Because of you and your filthy, furry friends, one of my customers is going to post a bad review online and THAT'S GOING TO HURT MY PROFITS!" Then a nasty smile creeps over her face. "Well, boy, if you like my smoothies so much, HAVE SOME OF THIS!"

All of a sudden Ms Fortune picks up the slops bin and tips it over Sean's head. The slop drops out like a slurry Niagara Falls.

SPLOOSH!

He is completely covered, dripping in old run-offs. Orange peel is glued to one cheek. The top of a pine-apple sits on top of his head like a gross fascinator.

We are all shocked, silent and still. Sean is too. Gloop drips from his eyebrows and the tip of his nose and splashes onto the floor. He looks like a melting candle. Those nearest to him shuffle away. He is, to be fair to them, absolutely disgusting. This is going to make school difficult for him. How can he be anything other than Sloppy Sean from now on.

TOTALLY DISGUSTING

"Disgusting!" spits Ms Fortune.

But then Sam steps forward. "Hey, Sean," he says. "Gimme five."

Sean stops. "Eh?" He looks at his own hands, dripping with food stuff.

"Come on," says Sam to Sean, ignoring Ms Fortune. He nods to his own clean palm.

"But…" says Sean, gesturing to his whole filthy body. "Look at me."

"Don't leave me hanging," says Sam, smiling.

"YOUNG MAN, DON'T YOU DARE GIVE HIM 'FIVE'. Don't give him anything!" shouts Ms Fortune. "Leave him!"

But Sean ignores her. He smiles and gives Sam a MASSIVE high five. The slap sends slop splurging out, speckling Sam in pink and brown splashback. But Sam just smiles. He pushes out his fist for the next step to the Acorn handshake.

"Really?" says Sean.

"Do it," says Sam. Sean bumps his fist into Sam's. More slop goes everywhere but Sam doesn't seem to mind. Next it's the ladder hands. This one they do much more quickly. Sloppy slop slops all over the shop.

| A double high five, | a shoulder-to-shoulder, | an elbow nudge. |

As they go through their routine, they get faster and faster. Slop is going everywhere. Sean is smiling too, laughing. It's hilarious. We're all laughing.

The handshake routine ends in a chest bump, everyone knows that. Surely they can't do the chest bump?

"STOP IT! STOP IT!" shouts Ms Fortune. But it's too late. They're going for it now. Slop is flying everywhere, but nobody seems to mind.

They do the chest bump SPLAT and now Sam is well and truly covered in slops too. There's a huge cheer. June whoops as she runs across the room and hurls

herself onto her knees, sliding on soggy stuff all over the floor like she's just scored a penalty in the World Cup final.

It's absolutely brilliant!

Within seconds, the whole hall is slip-sliding in slop. Rolling around, hooting with laughter. We're all throwing it at one another. Laughter and leftovers fill the air.

"STOP!" shouts Ms Fortune. She is powerless in the middle of the room.

Ms Perry is tottering about, trying to dodge the flying fruit.

"STOP THIS! STOP THIS RIGHT N—!" shouts Ms Fortune. She is cut short by a rotten kiwi fruit which hits her square in the forehead, leaving a splat of hairy goo between her eyebrows. A great cheer goes up!

24

RE-OPENING

I'm back at the dentist's for a check-up. After what happened yesterday with Ms Fortune and the rat-that-is-actually-Hammy and the walkie-talkies and the food fight, I'm glad not to be at school this morning. I'm still kind of freaked out about the way Ms Fortune looked at me after Ms Perry said I'd "heard" about the hamster. She can't have guessed what I can do, though, surely?

"Hi," I say as I take my seat in the old lime green dentist's chair. Fiona is at the little sink with her back to the room and doesn't answer. Why isn't she talking? Maybe she didn't hear me. I reach for the lever on the side of my chair to tip my head back – I go to the dentists loads, so I know the drill. Fiona steps round behind me and puts the plastic sheet over me, tying it down a bit tighter than usual.

And then she leans over me and I realize why Fiona isn't answering. She's not Fiona.

Not-Fiona has short grey hair poking from under his scrub cap and little round glasses under his goggles and a moustache like a broom. Hanging around his neck is a plastic mask. He really looks nothing like Fiona. What the walnut?

"I'm Mr Bridges," he says. His face is way too close and his breath smells like tuna mixed with summer fruits. "I'm your dentist for today. You could say I'm … filling in." He smiles. A dentist's teeth should be much whiter than this. His are yellow and rounded, like a line-up of Minions. He takes a big slurp from a disposable cup. A disposable cup labelled The Library.

NOT FIONA!

Something is fishy here, and not just this guy's breath.

"I'm not sure about this," I say, struggling against the plastic sheet. "I don't think I should... I, can we? I..."

"It's a good day for you, Thomasina J. Ginger," he says, ignoring me and leafing through his paperwork. "You're getting brand new braces. State of the art. Aren't you a lucky girl?"

"But I don't want new braces. I'm just fine with the ones I've got. Mum? Mum, tell him!"

"Be a good girl, angel," Mum says without looking up.

"This isn't right!" I say, panicking. "This is bad!"

"Nobody likes the dentist, sugarplum. It's just something you have to do, it's..." Mum frowns and starts tapping at her phone. "I got an email about

it this morning... Here it is... This is 'completely routine brace maintenance' it says. Then there's a thumbs up, so just lie back and be a good girl, yeah?"

Mail

Mum got the email this morning? But normally you get dentist appointments way in advance. Heat from the big light above me beats down. It's as hot and as bright as the sun on Mercury. Sweat pricks my brow. "I've got to go – I should really..."

"Just relax," says Mr Bridges, "and breathe deeply."

Breathe deeply? What the—?

Mr Bridges slips his mask up over his mouth and nose.

There is the snake hiss of a canister of laughing gas. A bitter taste, somewhere between candy floss and stainless steel. My mouth is dry. My eyelids heavy. The light is getting brighter. The ceiling is getting blurrier.

I am up in the clouds, floating. I am out in space.

I am in the sky with diamonds.

🦷 🦷 🦷

When I wake up I am still in the lime green dentist's chair. Mr Bridges is nowhere to be seen.

Mum is still here but she's slumped back in her chair. Her phone dangles from her hand.

I sit up slowly. The room spins. Something is wrong. Something is different. The room keeps spinning. Something is missing. Something is wrong.

I look about me,
and then I put my hand
to my mouth.
My braces …
I've got new braces.

I clench my teeth and hear nothing. Absolutely nothing. Oh no! I try not to panic. Maybe I can't hear anything because I'm too far away from school, out of range. Or maybe it might be because these new braces don't work in the same way.

Sweat pricks my brow all over again.

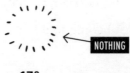

By the time I get to school it's already lunchtime. It always feels weird arriving when the whole school is in full swing but now I feel doubly odd.

STILL NOTHING!

I sneak into the playground and take my place in a quiet corner. What if that dentist has ruined my braces forever? I'll check again. I clench my teeth. There's nothing. My mouth is useless. I am useless.

Then Sam rushes up to me. "Where have you been!" he says.

"I was at the d—" I start.

"We've come up with a plan," Sam says urgently, cutting me off. Then voice dropping to a whisper, he adds, "We're going to rescue Hammy. We need you to help us – to keep us safe."

"I … no, I can't…" I start.

"You can! Hammy's in danger. We've got to get him back. Tonight. Eight o'clock. Meet at the gates. Don't be late. We can't talk again – all FAFF personnel are to stay separate today, just in case." Sam is rushing off again already.

"Wait!" I cry. "I can't." But it's too late. He's gone. What am I going to do?

25 PRINTS OF THIEVES

School looks different at night. It's … eerie, like it belongs on a movie poster for a horror film.

I had no problem sneaking out. Mum knows within five seconds if her phone is moved, but I could hitch-hike to Australia and get engaged to a koala and she wouldn't even know till we sent the wedding invitation.

Thomasina
&
a Koala
are getting married

I creep into the playground. I hope I see the others soon. I run my tongue over my teeth. I can taste metal and also, in a way, chicken. And by chicken I mean me. I am a chicken. Too much of a coward to tell the others about my new braces.

"Pssssst," someone is whispering. "Over here!" I follow the sound to where the others are hunched in the shadows of the main door.

"Hey!" says June.

"I'm so glad you're here!" says Adele. "I thought you might not come for a second. We couldn't do this without you."

"Or your braces..." says Nucky quietly.

I gulp, shivering slightly at the thought of what Ms Fortune will do if she catches us. And how powerless I am to save us.

FRIENDS
"They'll be there for you!"
30 day free trial

✁ cut out and keep

"Are you cold?" says Sam. He pulls off his hoody. "Here, wear this. I've got a spare." Underneath his hoody he is wearing … a second hoody. Classic Sam. "Feel better?" he says.

"Er … yeah, thanks," I say. He really cares about me. We're friends! All of us are. If I was waiting for a good time to tell them about the braces, this is it. But then … I might lose everything. I can't risk it. They could drop me like a hot tomato. I've had no friends for so long. It wouldn't be fair for me to lose them so soon. What is this, a free trial? "Let's go save that hamster," I say, assertively, leading the way. Me, leading a crack team through the darkness. Who'd have thunk it?

The main door to the building is locked.

Of course it is. We should have thought of that. Now what?

"Windows?" says Adele.

"You can't solve everything with computers," says Sam.

"No, the actual windows. Up there…" says Adele

patiently, pointing towards a set of windows to the side of the door. One of them is ajar.

"Oh."

After Nucky has used his parkour abilities to climb through the window (quite impressive … I guess) and open the door for us, we head through the darkness, towards the gold lift.

It seems shinier than ever in the gloomy corridor. Once we're inside, the robotic voice starts up, just like last time. "To proceed, please place a registered digit on the fingerprint scanning unit."

"I've got this," says Adele. She unfurls the Oak Tree poster from our classroom, the one that was pretty much ruined when Mr Price put his big fat fingerprint right in the middle of it.

She holds the fingerprint over the scanner panel. And … nothing happens. JUST KIDDING. It works a charm. The panel glows green dingle-dingle-ding.

"Good evening, Mr Price," says the lift. "This lift uses two-factor security. Please enter the alpha-numeric access code."

"Oh, beach balls," says Adele. She turns to me and Sam. "You didn't mention there was a password too. I thought it was just the fingerprint!"

"Sorry," we both mumble. "We forgot!"

"What now?!" says Nucky.

"Let's just think about it," I say. "What would Ms Fortune set as the password. What does she care about?"

"Well, not us, it turns out," says June. "Even though she said she did, at the start."

"She said all she cares about is, what was it ... moulding open nurtured educated youth," says Sam. "But that hardly helps – way too many letters. It's classic Ms Fortune business nonsense that means absolutely nothing."

"At the start ... Moulding Open Nurtured ..."
I repeat. "I think I've got it!"

I step up to the keypad. "At the start of *Moulding* ... M." I press the M key.

"At the start of *open*..." I press the O.

For each word, a letter. Soon enough:

All our headteacher cares about is money.

"Thank you," says the lift. "Going up."

26 CABINET RESHUFFLE

The lift doors slide open to reveal Ms Fortune's office. It is completely dark but for a blanket of moonlight coming through the big window.

"Let's find our hamster friend, shall we?" says Sam, tip toeing out into the gloom. We all follow, creeping like cat burglars.

We set to opening up every possible place he could be. June starts with the armoire. Adele goes to the bookcase. Between us we check in a cupboard, the desk drawers and behind an easel.

"Hammy Potter!" shouts Nucky, pulling open the filing cabinet. (I'm not entirely sure why we decided to do the search in alphabetical order.)

Nucky lifts out the Tupperware box. It has a couple of tiny holes in the top, like a salt cellar, and is wrapped in layer upon layer of that horrid grey tape. "He's in here!" Nucky says, tugging at the tape. We gather round as Nucky lifts our hamster out of the box. "Hammy!" he says excitedly.

He holds him aloft under his tiny arms like that bit at the start of the *Lion King*. He's tired and trembling, eyes dull. Dried poop dangles from his butt fur. (I'm talking about Hammy now, not Nucky.)

"Here you go, little dude," says Nucky, passing over a pumpkin seed from his pocket. "You're safe now."

Hammy takes the seed in his little hamster hands and immediately gets to work on his nibbling.

"Ahhhh," says June. "Hello, friend." She strokes his orange hamster head. Adele tickles his little hamster chin.

"What's this?" says Sam, peering into the open filing cabinet. He takes out a ring binder. A sticker on the front says "Ms F's secret plan, DO NOT READ".

"Oooh," says June.

June, Adele and I gather round behind Sam as he opens it up.

Business Plan
Please note - this is <u>TOP SECRET</u>

PHASE 1 ☑
Take over crummy school

PHASE 2 ☑
Close gym and open up a private spa

PHASE 3 ☑
Close library and open up a smoothie bar

PHASE 4 ☑
Sell school building to developers

PHASE 5 ☐
Use money from spa + bar + building = buy a YACHT!!!

PHASE 6 ☐
Spend rest of life cruising the world, drinking champagne and eating lobster sandwiches

"What the heck!" gasps June. "She's going to sell the whole school building!"

"Going to?" says Adele. She pulls out a sheet of paper from further through the binder. "The sale's gone through already. This building now belongs to 'Luxcorp© Assets'."

"It just needs the council sign-off, and then it's done," says Sam, reading over Adele's shoulder.

"Luxcorp what-now?" says Nucky.

"They're property developers," says Adele. "They buy up buildings and kick out people and sell them on for a big profit. As soon as this goes through, we're homeless. Well, school-less."

"There's a load of brochures for Hawaii here too," adds June. "Ms Fortune obviously isn't planning on sticking around. Look." The brochure is reflected in the window: ⸮THƆAY TAHW. Wait a minute: Thcay Tahw … I remember it from the first time I was in here. I spin round to read the title on the brochure: What Yacht?

"Our headteacher is an evil genius!" says Sam, flicking through a brochure. "And that binder has all the proof we need!"

"Squeak, squeak, squeak," says Hammy Potter, coming back to his old self. It's probably hamster language for "Thanks for rescuing me, guys!"

"Squeak, squeak, SQUEAK!" he says, his eyes widening. It's probably hamster language for "No, REALLY thank you so much!" Although it's a bit more desperate than that. And he appears to be looking over our shoulders.

We finally turn to see we are not alone. It's Mr Pin. "I'll take THAT," he says, plucking the binder from Adele's hands. He turns on his heels. Behind him is the shredder. He pushes the contents of the binder inside.

"The evidence!" shouts June.

Paper shreds are blown in the air like tiny autumn leaves. They are cream and ivory (invoices, contracts), they are glossy golds and bright blues (brochures). They are scraps. Useless scraps.

"NooooOOOooo!" we all shout.

Sam turns to me. "Didn't you know he was here?" he hisses. "Why didn't you warn us!?"

"I ... I ... " I say, as I watch Nucky carefully drop Hammy into his shirt pocket. "They, er, they must use different radio frequencies at night time," I mumble.

"And what about Mr Price!?" says June urgently. "Is he here too?"

"I am!" says a voice behind us, making us jump. But before we can properly react, another weird sound

CCCCCRRRRRRRPPPPTTTT

and then we are caught up in something strong and sticky. Flipping grey tape! And wrapping it round and round us, that flipping great ape: Mr Price! Suddenly we are stuck. Five flies trapped in a web.

"Hey!"   "Stop!"   "Oi!"

"You kids were clever getting in here, but you can't outsmart Ms Fortune. She's a super head! In comparison you guys are super ... stupid," says Mr Price.

There's nothing we can do. We're trapped. Bound up like tree trunks ready for the wood chipper. Mr Pin finishes the whole roll of tape and then Mr Price comes over with a thick rope, which he ties tight round the middle of us. Then he pushes us over onto our sides. Mr Pin opens the big window and together they push and lift us out onto the sill. The cool night air rushes over us and then we are – and this is just so wrong – we are defenestrated. And if you don't know what that means, it means that they ACTUALLY CHUCK US OUT OF THE ACTUAL WINDOW!

Defenestration – try to use it in a sentence today. I probably won't, because I'm too busy being stuck to my friends, falling to my death.

We fall down
       down
          down towards the concrete playground,
miles below.

We fall for what feels like – well, actually, not very long tbh. Less than a second. We don't even have time to scream before we hit something hard and woody.

We've landed on scaffolding.

We don't stop there. The wooden planks are angled downwards and we are a rolling bundle of humanity that can't stop, won't stop.

And then the planks end, and there is nothing. We are still spinning. We are falling. There's a bright light. Is it … heaven? Am I dead??

We crash down onto another surface. It's black. It's sticky. It's … fruity? Where are we? The room seems incredibly bright.

"Hello, children," says a voice. Ms Fortune hisses slowly upwards on a platform on wheels, like a snake lifting its head from a basket.

This can't be good.

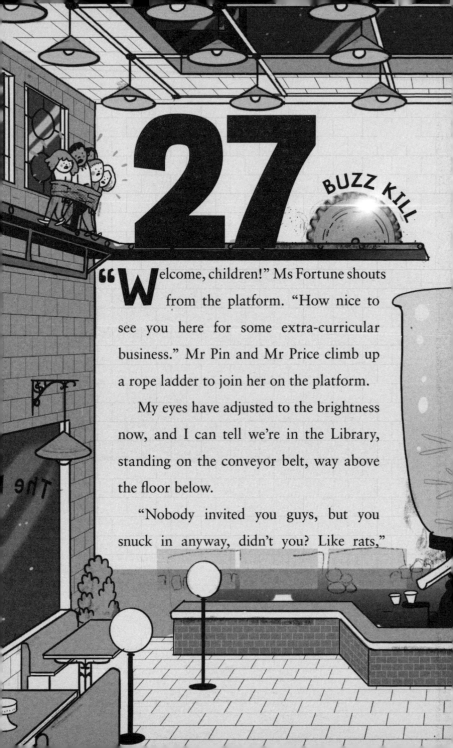

27

BUZZ KILL

"**W**elcome, children!" Ms Fortune shouts from the platform. "How nice to see you here for some extra-curricular business." Mr Pin and Mr Price climb up a rope ladder to join her on the platform.

My eyes have adjusted to the brightness now, and I can tell we're in the Library, standing on the conveyor belt, way above the floor below.

"Nobody invited you guys, but you snuck in anyway, didn't you? Like rats,"

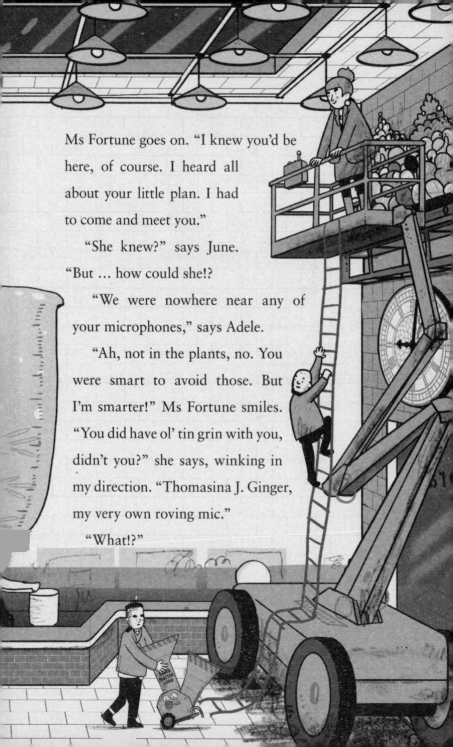

Ms Fortune goes on. "I knew you'd be here, of course. I heard all about your little plan. I had to come and meet you."

"She knew?" says June. "But ... how could she!?

"We were nowhere near any of your microphones," says Adele.

"Ah, not in the plants, no. You were smart to avoid those. But I'm smarter!" Ms Fortune smiles. "You did have ol' tin grin with you, didn't you?" she says, winking in my direction. "Thomasina J. Ginger, my very own roving mic."

"What!?"

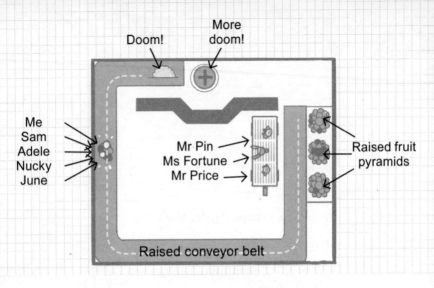

"That's right! I know everything. When Ms Perry said that Thomasina had 'heard' all about the rat in the Library, I was suspicious. So I sent Serge and Chip into your classroom after-hours and they found this nice drawing. Very impressive. 'Diode.'" Ms Fortune holds up a scrap of paper in a plastic wallet. It's Adele's diagram of the braces, from my exercise book. How could we have been so careless? "It's all very clear. I understood right away. Enough even to adapt the science for my own use. I got a nice dentist to fit Tom out with a new pair of braces. We reverse-engineered the tech so that Tom's braces allowed us to listen in to you guys. That's how I knew you'd be here tonight."

"What?!" says Sam.

"No!" says Adele. "You didn't!"

"How are you finding your upgraded braces by the way, Thomasina?"

"They changed your braces?" says Sam. "And you didn't tell us?"

"Why, Tom?" snaps Adele. She's angry, of course. They all are.

"I … I … I…" I stammer.

"That old shyness came back, did it?" says Ms Fortune. "I knew it would! People never change. Apart from me. I'm rich now, I'll be changing all the time! Changing out of this basic suit and into Versace, Gucci, Prada and all the other things that mega-rich people wear on their mega-yachts. There's just one last piece of unfinished business before we leave. You guys."

Ms Fortune jabs the big green button on a control panel. Below us the conveyor belt starts to move, taking us slowly towards the the buzzsaw which now starts to spin faster and faster. We're just a few metres away from being buzzed, sawed and blitzed to death.

"You can't do this," shouts Nucky. "What about our parents!? They'll be in bits!"

"No, no." Ms Fortune laughs. "You will. Your parents will be absolutely fine. I'll just say you five are on a French exchange trip! And by the time they start to get worried I'll be a long, long way away."

We're nearer to the metal blades now. Closer and closer to the blender. To our doom.

Nucky's beanbag-with-a-face is a bit further down the conveyor belt. It must have come out of his pocket when we landed. The beanbag is carried along onto the spinning blade of the buzzsaw. In a flash it is all over. A has-been. The sweet orange bag is transformed into a horrid mess of stuffing and scraps of fabric. Beads spill in all directions. Then the gruesome remains fall down onto the whizzing blades below. The sound is horrible. Can beanbags scream? Orange scraps and stuffing puff into the air.

Everything we've managed – it was all down to my weird braces. And now what am I good for? Absolutely nothing. The others are still straining to get unstuck, but I've given up. I'll go the way of that beanbag. Let the big blender turn me to pulp. Maybe I'll do better as a smoothie? Maybe I'll live on in a cup, someone's tummy, their guts, pass through their bum hole. I'll be a turd in a loo and then flushed and then, finally, lost in the endless abyss of the ocean. It doesn't sound so bad, in a way.

In about twelve seconds I'm going to die surrounded by friends. I didn't even have friends before. Perhaps that was for the best. I mean, I always wanted to blend in more ... but not like this.

BUZZZZZZ!

A gust of chill night air hits me as we travel past a smashed window. It's the window I smashed at the start of all this. Who knew I could throw that Frisbee so far? The sight of it reminds me of how lonely I was back then. I don't want to go back to being awkward old Tom, But then I don't want to be new smoothie Tom either. Then I see something familiar up ahead. Down the side of the conveyor belt like a forgotten Christmas decoration is a jolly red disc. "My Frisbee!" says Sam.

It must have been here the whole time! It looks like a giant record icon and that gives me an idea. I wheedle my hand round to my pocket. I pull out Mum's old phone and, keeping it low,

Voice memos

DOES THIS RING
A BELL??

I open up the voice recorder app and press RECORD.

"But, Ms Fortune, you'll never get away with it!" I shout, running my tongue over my new braces nervously.

"What are you doing?" whispers Sam.

"Get away with it? Ha! I already have!" Ms Fortune says. "This town has got a new hotel! Or casino. Or block of flats. Whatever! It's up to the developers. The point is, I've been paid. I've got a suitcase full of money and I'm off to buy a super yacht. Meanwhile, you're going to be blitzed to death. And all because you don't have Tom's magic braces any more." She gives an evil cackle.

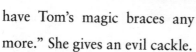

SOLID GOLD!

"She's wrong," I say, quietly.

"You mean ... we're not going to die!?" says Nucky, a glimmer of hope in his voice. "We won't get blitzed to death?"

"Er ... no, that's probably true," I say. The sounds of the machinery are getting louder and louder. "What I mean is, she's wrong to say that everything we've done was because of the braces! Think about it: The posters! The pants! The fingerprint! The plan to rescue Hammy... None of that was the braces. It was us. We did it – together!"

"It's true!" says Sam. He's smiling now. "It was all of us! It was—"

"TEAMWORK!" says Sam, Adele, June and Nucky in unison. "FAFF!" I shout at exactly the same time. I … I'll get there next time.

"That's what we need now," I say. "To work together."

"Do you have a plan?" Adele asks.

I nod. A sort of plan. A half plan. A *pl.* "First we need to stop this conveyor belt. If we can grab that Frisbee, when we get to it I can probably chuck it into the red STOP button. Nucky, do you think Hammy can bite through this tape?" I whisper.

"What are you kids talking about over there?" Ms Fortune shouts from her platform. The whirring giant blender means she can't quite hear us.

"Just about how it's all over for us…!" I shout, before whispering to the others, "she can't hear us over the machinery. Nucky, get Hammy. Put him to work! We need that Frisbee." I threw the Frisbee so far that day I broke the library window. I totally smashed it. Can I do it again now?

Nucky wiggles his shoulders to shake Hammy up from his shirt pocket. I feel tiny hands and feet on my arms as Hammy chews on the tape. My arm is free! I stretch out as far as I can towards the Frisbee, snatching it up as we go past it, just in time.

And then I try to focus. I look hard at the red STOP button, take a deep breath and flick my wrist forwards.

FLING.

The Frisbee sails out towards the big red button. But then it turns upwards. Oh no! I missed! Up and on the Frisbee flies, past the big red button that was going to save us all. Rats.

28 FRUIT DROPS

Up and on the Frisbee flies, past the big red button. Instead it smashes into the fruit pyramid behind Ms Fortune's platform. Oranges tumble down. And they're not the only fruit – soon there's a technicolour avalanche of smoothie ingredients. Oranges and lemons, satsumas and melons rain down on Ms Fortune, Mr Pin and Mr Price. It looks like expert-mode on Fruit Ninja.

"Ow, ow, ow, ow, OW!"

The Frisbee didn't do exactly what I'd been planning, but at least they're distracted and now we can try and get out of this tape. Hammy could chew through the tape around our arms, but next we have to get out of this thick rope.

"June," I shout. "We need you now – untie us! Quickly. It's a giant, life-or-death version of cat's cradle."

June frowns, shrugs, and sets to work, her fingers picking at the knot. "HOLD THIS!" she says to Sam, passing him one end of the tape. "PUT YOUR FINGER HERE," she tells Adele. "TAKE THIS END," she tells me. "AND ... EVERYONE TWIST!" We follow June's instructions and all at once we're free. The loose rope drops around our feet like old spaghetti. Not that we can go anywhere – there is a brick wall to one side of us, a massive drop to the other.

Ms Fortune, Mr Pin and Mr Price are still buried in a great fruit salad. "We'll have to press the button manually," says Adele.

Nucky eyes the control panel. It is high up too, and way across the other side of the library. It's also right by

the fruit mountain covering Ms Fortune and the others.

"Use your parkour!" I say. "Now's your time!"

Nucky grins and then launches himself at one of the fancy lights hanging above us. He swings, Tarzan-style, from one light to another. He lets go of the last light and lands like a gymnast on the metal railing of Ms Fortune's platform. He drops down right by the control panel. Holy macadamia! It's like Super Mario meets Ninja Warrior.

"He's made it!" said June.

"Thank FLIP for parkour!" says Sam.

I glance ahead of us. The spinning blades of the blender are about a metre away now. A few more seconds and the blades will slice us up like human

salami. The buzzing sound is almost unbearable.

"Hurry, Nucky!" Adele shouts. Nucky swings his arm over his head like Thor's hammer and smacks it down on the big red button.

BZZZZZZZ–CRACK-GRRR

There is the crunch of metal on metal as the conveyor belt comes to a stuttering halt. We are millimetres from the edge of the first robot blade. We're safe!

Well, three of us are. Nucky is in clear and present peril. Ms Fortune is clambering out of the pile of fruit, Mr Pin and Mr Price are already out. And poor Nucky is right in the middle of them – a Nucky sandwich!

29 BIG REACTION

"**Y**ou stinking RAT!" shouts Ms Fortune. She has a banana skin on her head and fruit juice all over her. She's still holding her can of cola (which I have to admit is pretty impressive). "Get him!"

Mr Pin swipes at Nucky, but Nucky is too fast. He ducks out of the way and is about to – *whoops!* – oh no! He slips on a banana skin. I thought that only happened in stupid books! His foot slides forward and his body flies backwards, landing him squarely in the arms of Mr Pin.

Ms Fortune is on her feet now, orange peel sliding down her face. "Oh, you're going to regret that, Nicky!" she says nastily. She's furious. "Serge – the shredder!" Mr Price immediately fires up the SHREDMASTER 3000. It comes to life with its horrific screeching sound. Mr Pin drags Nucky towards it.

"It's Nucky!" shouts Nucky. "NUCKY!" He fusses and fights as much as he can, but Mr Pin has him held tight.

They are actually going to shred him! All we can do from way over on the conveyor belt is watch. Nucky is doing everything he can to escape but it's no use. He kicks backwards towards Mr Pin and hits his jacket pocket. A bunch of little balls scatters on the platform floor.

WEIRD TINY BALLS

A MENTO
(OTHER SCOTCH MINTS
ARE AVAILABLE)

"What were those white things?" says Sam.

"They look like …. they are. Mentos!" says June. "That's it! Use the Mentos, Nucky!" she shouts. "They're still in Mr Pin's pocket – get one in the can!"

Nucky looks back to us, frowning. "In the can!" shouts June. All of a sudden, Nucky catches on. His expression becomes one of resolve as he manages to work a hand behind him and into Mr Pin's jacket pocket. He pulls out a fist full of mints just as he is being dragged past Ms Fortune. This is his last chance! He stamps down on Mr Pin's toes, and the shock of it means his arm is free enough to try to get some of the sweets into Ms Fortune's drink.

Nucky tosses the mints.

The next bit all seems to happen in slow motion. A couple of the mints ping off to the side, like a flock of tiny doves. But most of them make it in. There's a beat. Ms Fortune's eyes widen with horror as her drink starts to froth and bubble. Then everything speeds up again. Right up.

A BOOM! shake-shake-shakes the room. The explosive combination of Mentos and diet cola causes a huge brown plume of foam to jet right into Ms Fortune's stupid face.

SPLOOSH!

"GAAH!"
she shouts as a pair of glasses are blasted from her head. It must be powerful stuff – Ms Fortune doesn't even wear glasses.

She topples backwards, arms flailing like a dying octopus.

The sticky brown jet keeps on pumping out, sending her hair wild and blasts away her winky walkie-talkie badge. She slams back into Mr Price and somehow her cuff gets caught in the shredder.

SKKKRREEEEEEEEEEEEEE

says the shredder as it tears into Ms Fortune's jacket.

"EEEEEEEEEEEK!" shrieks Ms Fortune. Her arm is dragged down towards the metal mouth. Her can crunches into the machinery, sending sparks flying.

Mr Pin lets go of Nucky to help her. He grabs Ms Fortune's other arm and yanks it back, setting her free.

"That's IT!"

she screams. "I've had enough of this nonsense."

Ms Fortune is sopping with soda, speckled with fruit chunks, raggedy as a hobo. "Forget about the kids! We've got the money. Get me out of here!" She clambers down from the platform and runs out through the library door. Mr Price and Mr Pin follow close behind.

"Quick!" I shout. "They're getting away."

Nucky steers the cherry picker platform over to us but by the time we've all clambered on, we're too late. We hear the engine of the limousine, the squeal of tyres, honking horns in the distance.

SQUEAL

HONK

HONK

HON

BELL DE JOUR

"It's too late." says Sam. "We missed our chance. They're gone and we've got no evidence."

"Haven't we?" I say, holding up Mum's phone. "I recorded Ms Fortune gloating. It's all the evidence we need."

"Yeah, but ... we need people to hear it," says June.

"Couldn't we use this thing?" says Nucky. He picks up Ms Fortune's smiley-face badge from the floor. I take it from him. It's sticky with cola. I turn it over in my hand.

There's a little switch on the back with two settings. TWO-WAY and OUTGOING. I push it to outgoing. I lean towards it, putting the tiny microphone to my mouth, "Hello" I whisper. A crackly "HELLO" is relayed out of the PA system speakers all round the room. It's loud, but not nearly loud enough.

I sigh and look up at the stars through the library skylight. Silhouetted against the dark sky is the school bell. And then – boom! – "I have an idea," I say to the others.

It only takes me a few moments to explain what I want to do. Which is good, because we need to move quickly. Adele takes over the controls of the cherry picker as we use it to gather the intercom speakers from around the room. Then she takes us up towards the ceiling.

Nucky hits the button for the retractable roof. The skylight peels back to reveal the starry sky above us. We go through the open roof, finally stopping beside the large school bell. We put all the speakers inside it.

"It's the biggest boom-bowl ever!" says Sam.

"Face them into the bell," says Adele. "It's a parabolic reflector – the sound will reflect out, towards the town."

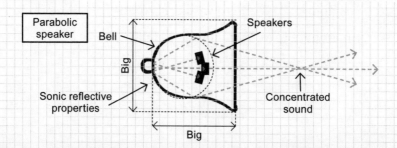

"Will it be louder?" says Nucky.

"There's only one way to find out."

I hand Sam the badge. "Do it, Sam. Tell them everything."

"Me?" Sam smiles. "This is all you. You've got this."

I'm so high, up with the stars.

I can see the whole of Belton sprawling out into the dark valley in front of us. There's a cool night breeze.

I feel surprisingly calm.

I close my eyes and hold the badge up to my mouth. I clear my throat – ha hum. "HA HUM!" roars out of our big bell speaker.

"It's working!" says Adele. "It's really working!"

"Um… Hello!" I continue. My voice booms out towards the town. The last syllable echoes into the dark night sky like HELLO-O-o-o-o-ᴏ-

"Keep going," urges Sam.

"Hello!" I say again. "My name is Tom. Er, Thomasina Ginger. I am a pupil at Belton Primary. Our headteacher, Ms Fortune, is evil. She is a criminal. She's tricked all of you so that she could get money for herself. Just listen to this…"

I hold the phone up by the microphone in the badge and press PLAY. Ms Fortune's voice booms out from the the bell. *"The school is over. I've sold everything! I'm going to buy a yacht!"* she says.

The whole town is dark, but then a bright square appears. A light in a window. Just one at first, then a second. A couple more.

"She's destroyed our whole school, and taken all your money. And now she's on her way to the airport to escape to Hawaii. Stop her!" My words ring out across the town. More lights come on. Before long it's a pixelated galaxy.

"It's working!" says Adele. "They've heard you, Tom." Sam puts his hand on her shoulder and smiles at me. June and Nucky are smiling too. We all look out to Belton together. I keep talking, and play more of Ms Fortune's speech.

More lights. Not just the ⬚, ⬚⬚ and ⬚ shapes of windows now, but the growing o o of car headlights too. Glowing and growing as they come towards us.

"It's worked, Tom!" says Adele.

"We've been heard!!" says June. "They're coming!"

"The police are coming, too," says Nucky, peering out at approaching flashing blue lights in the distance.

I keep talking. I tell them everything. With my friends behind me, I don't want to stop.

31

#TRENDING

EVIL HEAD CAUGHT
DASTARDLY PLOT FOILED BY MEDDLING KIDS

DETENTION!
SCHEMING HEADTEACHER SENT TO PRISON

HEADMONSTER!
MS FORTUNE TOOK MONEY FOR HERSELF

BAD GUYS HATE HER!
Local kid exposes shocking truth with this one weird trick
>>Click here

KIDS ARE ALL RIGHT
SCHOOLCHILDREN PRAISED BY POLICE

I didn't actually see what happened to Ms Fortune, but I got to read all about it. Pretty much everyone did. It was front-page news around the world and was Belton's number one trending topic on Twitter for six and a half days. (Until Tim Holmes's pet pug had puppies. #TheHolmesPack were pretty cute.)

I didn't speak much to Mum about the whole thing, but I noticed that pretty much every article I saw had comments from GingerNinja_88...

GingerNinja_88 8m ago
She's just the best child in the world. 10/10! ☺
>>Reply

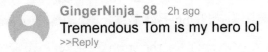

GingerNinja_88 2h ago
Tremendous Tom is my hero lol
>>Reply

GingerNinja_88 6h ago
IM SO PROUD ☺☺☺☺☺☺
>>Reply

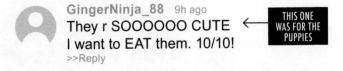

GingerNinja_88 9h ago
They r SOOOOOO CUTE ← THIS ONE WAS FOR THE PUPPIES
I want to EAT them. 10/10!
>>Reply

Also she started hugging me a lot more. And when she did I felt invincible.

So that was nice.

32 ALMOST OVER NOW

So that was that. It was ages ago now. I can barely believe it all happened. I'd probably think it was a dream if it weren't for the special stickers we were sent by Roy Turner, the mayor of Belton.

Ms Fortune was sent to prison! All of her assets were transferred to the school, so we got a completely new library (a proper one, with books!) in the end. We also got to keep the spa building and have inherited Ms Fortune's limousine (mostly used by the netball team). We also got about 400 cans of cola and 14 ladies' suits.

And of course we needed a new headteacher. Mr Hooper didn't answer any of the emails, and so they offered the job to Mr Ward!

• • •

Everyone's happy.

Even Hammy Potter is happy. A crop of pumpkins popped up from the seeds we scattered at his memorial service, so he has an unlimited supply of snacks.

I've got no braces now. That's finished too. The weird thing, though, is that without braces, I still feel the same. I spent so long imagining myself without them, I thought I'd be a different person. But now I feel kind of the same as I always did. Maybe, somewhere deep inside, I've switched a little switch towards OUTGOING, but I'm pretty much as I was before. But it's not so bad. In fact, I quite like it.

THE END

WHAT ABOUT MR HOOPER?

Mr Hooper
Pickleholic

Oh, I almost forgot to mention – Mr Hooper!

We found him in the end, several weeks later. It turned out he was locked in the Old Shed the whole time. Luckily it was used as a canteen store cupboard in the 1980s and he shared it with crates and crates of pickled gherkins so didn't go hungry (he ate the pickles) or thirsty (he drank the pickle juice).

PS He STINKS of pickles.

YOU HAVE BEEN READING

MY HEADTEACHER IS AN EVIL GENIUS

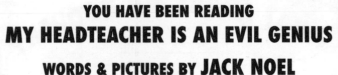

WORDS & PICTURES BY JACK NOEL

EDITD BY ANNALIE GRAINGER & MARA BERGMAN

COPY-EDITING HELEN MORTIMER

ART-DIRECTION BEN NORLAND

PRODUCTION SARAH PARKER

FOREIGN RIGHTS KAREN COEMAN, LARA ARMSTRONG & GIANLUCA DICRISTOFARO ALFARO

ED RIPLEY AND THE ENTIRE WALKER BOOKS SALES & MARKETING TEAM

PUBLISHER DENISE JOHNSTONE-BURT

AGENT CLAIRE WILSON

SPECIAL THANKS CHARLOTTE KNIGHT

NO ANIMALS WERE HARMED IN THE MAKING OF THIS BOOK.
SADLY SOME TREES DID HAVE TO GIVE THEIR LIVES.

JACK WOULD LIKE YOU TO KNOW THAT IT IS TOTALLY TRUE, APPARENTLY,
THAT PEOPLE CAN PICK UP RADIO WAVES ON THEIR BRACES.